I0720606

ANDREA PALLADIO

THE ARCHITECT
WHO CHANGED OUR WORLD

Pamela Winfrey

Barbera Foundation, Inc.
P.O. Box 1019
Temple City, CA 91780

Copyright © 2020 Barbera Foundation, Inc.
Cover front photo: MB_Photo / Alamy Stock Photo
                    Chris Selby / Alamy Stock Photo
Cover design: Suzanne Turpin

More information at www.mentorisproject.org

ISBN: 978-1-947431-32-4

Library of Congress Control Number: 2020952147

All net proceeds from the sale of this book will be donated to Barbera Foundation, Inc. whose mission is to support educational initiatives that foster an appreciation of history and culture to encourage and inspire young people to create a stronger future.

The Mentoris Project is a series of novels and biographies about the lives of great men and women who have changed history through their contributions as scientists, inventors, explorers, thinkers, and creators. The Barbera Foundation sponsors this series in the hope that, like a mentor, each book will inspire the reader to discover how she or he can make a positive contribution to society.

Contents

Foreword

First and foremost, Mentor was a person. We tend to think of the word *mentor* as a noun (a mentor) or a verb (to mentor), but there is a very human dimension embedded in the term. Mentor appears in Homer's *Odyssey* as the old friend entrusted to care for Odysseus's household and his son Telemachus during the Trojan War. When years pass and Telemachus sets out to search for his missing father, the goddess Athena assumes the form of Mentor to accompany him. The human being welcomes a human form for counsel. From its very origins, becoming a mentor is a transcendent act; it carries with it something of the holy.

The Mentoris Project sets out on an Athena-like mission: We hope the books that form this series will be an inspiration to all those who are seekers, to those of the twenty-first century who are on their own odysseys, trying to find enduring principles that will guide them to a spiritual home. The stories that comprise the series are all deeply human. These books dramatize the lives of great men and women whose stories bridge the ancient and the modern, taking many forms, just as Athena did, but always holding up a light for those living today.

Whether in novel form or traditional biography, these

books plumb the individual characters of our heroes' journeys. The power of storytelling has always been to envelop the reader in a vivid and continuous dream, and to forge a link with the subject. Our goal is for that link to guide the reader home with a new inspiration.

What is a mentor? A guide, a moral compass, an inspiration. A friend who points you toward true north. We hope that the Mentoris Project will become that friend, and it will help us all transcend our daily lives with something that can only be called holy.

—Robert J. Barbera, Founder, The Mentoris Project
—Ken LaZebnik, Founding Editor, The Mentoris Project

*Dedicated to my mother, Alexa, who knows
how to walk through the woods.*

Chapter One

1508: ANDREA'S BIRTH

Marta gazed at the geranium petal in the palm of her hand. It was the color of blood. The color of the ribbon her own mother had worn in her hair. The color of sacrifice and pain, joy and the richness of life. So much to observe in a single petal of a single flower plucked from the one flowerpot on her own singular balcony. She sighed, allowing the petal to drop from her hand and out the open window where it caught the light for a moment before disappearing.

With effort, she crossed to the rough wooden table. Marta was a woman who would not be defined by a limp even though her limp was more pronounced now that she was about to give birth. She knew who she was and what she could do. She was one of the best seamstresses in Padua, she was wife to a wise man who was a miller, and she was going to give birth to a beautiful child that she would love and nurture; a person who would change the world. That was the way her mind worked.

Childbirth was frightening, true, but so was much of life. *If you let it scare you, it defeated you*, she thought as she continued to wash up after breakfast. Their apartment was small with only one bedroom, but it was on the third floor, so when she opened the shutters in the morning, the sunlight poured into the room and warmed the white stone floor so it, too, was emitting light.

She always made sure to keep geraniums and roses outside the window so that their red and pink petals could always be seen when the shutters were open. She put her elbows on the windowsill and watched as the chittering swallows swooped by. She smelled a faint fishy whiff from the Brenta River and the curious smell that wafted from her husband's mill nearby.

Suddenly, Pietro appeared, surprising her, making her jump a little. He came up behind her and hugged as much of her as he could, for it seemed that during the last few days, she had increased twofold in size. He, too, was worried, for women died from childbirth so often. Everything would go well, and then afterward, they seemed to sicken and die. *God will provide*, he thought, and crossed himself. It was the thirtieth of November, the Feast Day of Saint Andrew the Apostle. If both his wife and child survived, Pietro would call the child Andrea after the saint.

As it turned out, there was never such an easy baby to birth as Andrea di Pietro della Gondola, for he slid into the world effortlessly. For Marta, it was easier than so many things—washing the parquet floors that belonged to her mistress, the Lady Bossiglio, or sewing a thousand pearls into her best dress. Or listening to Lady Bossiglio's mother drone on endlessly about the problems between the papal powers in Rome and the rulers of

Venice. Every day she would cross herself, look fearfully around the room, and shriek, "They will be here any day now! The wars will come to Padua and blood will be painted upon our door!" Marta had been prepared for the worst, for it was a tradition for experienced mothers to scare the expectant mother with war stories of their own, the stories of the blood of giving birth.

The boy was so tiny that he fit into the crux of Pietro's arm. He had dark curly hair and a quiet, watchful way about him. Marta was worried that he would not last a day—he was so silent and small, he seemed to take up a sort of negative space. She could fold his ears for they were as pliable as velvet and lacked any cartilage. For months, Marta instinctively kept him home. She breastfed him and kept him warm, since November could be a month of chills and drafts. She made certain that he stayed close to the fire.

Pietro continued to go to the mill, and because of this, the family always had fresh milled grain for bread. Slowly, they began to accept visitors at home. His uncle Lucca, the boatman, visited. He always smelled of water and mud, and had a way of making each room he entered seem small. Lucca would tell them of his latest passengers and the stories they told as they flowed down the river. He'd heard it all—happy marriages, unhappy boys; solid, healthy minds and those that were broken by some insidious war; people who loved life and people who were ready to leave it. Marta, with her studied ways, took it all in with a small smile as she continued to care for her precious Andrea, and Pietro would slap his thigh in response.

A year and a half passed. Marta loved her domestic life. The wondrous nature of a child filled the rooms with all of the complexities of a young life. Andrea was a watchful boy, seemingly aware of all that went on in his parents' lives. Marta noticed that when Pietro held him and his head peeped over his father's shoulders, Andrea looked like a cat after a full bowl of milk, sated and safe.

But now, the sweetness of her home clashed horribly with the streets of Padua. As Lady Bossiglio's mother had predicted, it was under siege. Marta and Pietro spent many evenings trying to understand what had transformed their peaceful city. They sat in front of the fire, Andrea asleep in Marta's arms, and pored over the details. Prior to this year, Padua had been under Venetian rule and most Paduans were bonded both economically and spiritually with nearby Venice.

Marta's murmuring voice carried an edge to it. "Rome is as far away as the moon. I don't understand why they think they can invade us as though we were . . ." and then she hesitated, thinking, *English!*

Pietro, too, carried a black spot in his heart for Rome. He blamed Pope Julius and called him "the fool who designated that idiot Maximilian" as Holy Roman Emperor. Maximilian was part of the League of Cambrai, an anti-Venice alliance made up of Pope Julius, Louis XII of France, and Ferdinand II of Aragon. And Pietro felt that Maximilian would do anything, everything to make a name for himself.

He had not been far wrong, for Maximilian captured the city in June. Venetian forces responded with fury and marched from Treviso under the command of Andrea Gritti, who had been sent by the powerful Council of Ten who ruled Venice. Gritti brought with him *stradioti*, professional mercenaries from the Balkans. In turn, Maximilian had hired *landsknechts*, German professional soldiers. This resulted in the streets ringing with strident voices that could be heard crying and dying in a rainbow of languages.

The town was like a field fire with areas that would flare up and die down. One never knew when a skirmish would erupt, when a hot spot that had been smoldering unseen would break out. This made everyday life especially dangerous, for one could be convinced that all was well and then turn the corner to be plunged into the middle of a battle.

Pietro managed to keep the mill in operation sporadically, responding to people who, sometimes dodging bullets, managed to bring some grain to be ground. Unlike in times of peace, they could only bring as much as they could carry, for if they brought a cart drawn by a sturdy ox, chances are the ox and the cart would be commandeered, and the farmer would not be able to make a living.

Chapter Two

1510–1515: WAR AMONG THE TOYS

1510

Andrea, although only two years old, was obsessed with wooden blocks. He spent hours stacking them, and he would cry when the vibrations of the cannon, only a mile off, would shake the foundations enough to make them fall. But Andrea was already tenacious; time and time again, the blocks would fall, and time and time again, he would set them up again, as patient as an old man.

He looked up, for the sculptor Vincenzo Grandi had come through the door. His godfather. To Andrea he was a giant. From his perspective, Vincenzo was all looming belly and ringing voice. Everything he did was large. Vincenzo scooped him up and lifted him up over his head and high into the air. He squeezed Andrea like an accordion, and Andrea whooshed out a laugh. Marta looked up from stirring her pot and smiled indulgently, for Vincenzo was a trusted friend.

Vincenzo took his job of being Andrea's godfather seriously. He often brought the child over to his sculpture studio and allowed Andrea to run his hands over the half-finished sculptures. Andrea was careful and respectful, understanding that the shapes beneath his hands were in process and needed to be treated with care. Vincenzo used to joke that the statues were like small boys; if they were treated with care, they would grow up to be works of art.

Pietro and Vincenzo were good friends and had been since the early days before Pietro had started a family. Vincenzo had been honored when Pietro had asked him to be Andrea's godfather. Vincenzo made certain that Andrea was well versed in the merits of sculpture, painting, frescoes, and pottery. He had him plunge his hands into clay and challenged him to shape ducks, trees, and nutrias, the large mammals that frequented the rivers.

That Christmas season, on January 6, the Epiphany, Andrea surprised him with a small clay sculpture. Vincenzo could not see what it was intended to be until Andrea explained that it was a sculpture of Vincenzo himself. For once, Vincenzo did not respond with a roar, but instead examined the gift carefully, respectfully. He asked Andrea about his choice of materials, to which Andrea answered "Clay." He asked him about the color and Andrea said "Gray." He asked him where his nose was and Andrea grabbed Vincenzo's real nose so hard that it made tears spring to Vincenzo's eyes. That was when his roaring laugh erupted.

Marta served another small glass of wine to both Pietro and Vincenzo in celebration of a beautiful Christmas free of fighting in the city. She raised a glass to Vincenzo, thanking him, for like the Magi, he had brought the family many gifts.

Andrea adored going to the mill with his father for it was a secret place that most people were not allowed to enter. Due to the secrets of the trade, Pietro, like most millers, made the farmers stay outside with their horses and carts while their grain was being ground. Only the workers, the hopper boy, and the mill's calico cat were allowed in.

Each morning, the mill sat quiet. Pietro and Andrea would unlock the massive oak door and stand in the middle of the yawning space. The sun found its way down in shafts and the motes of dust and grain would make them look as though you could slide down them. The space contained a multitude of small noises—scampering mice; shifting, creaking slabs of wood; the fluttering of wings high in the rooftop. But when the lever was pulled and the water began to fill the buckets on the wheel, the place sprang alive with sound. There was such a loud collection of watery noises that Andrea always felt a little afraid, because he sometimes had nightmares about drowning. The reluctant creaking of the wheel reminded him of bones and the gritty sounds of the millstones, scraping heavily against each other, sometimes made the hairs on the back of his neck crawl.

The day truly began with the bell, announcing that someone was at the door ready with grain. The workers would jump to their positions, for each one had a job to do and they knew that without their contributions, the mill would not function.

The mill was a place of conversation as waiting was inevitable. Pietro knew everyone: Father Lorenzo's baker; the sisters at the Saint Anthony cloister; the militia's cook, Giancarlo; and the seven-year-old who worked at the bakery next door and was the one responsible for fetching flour. Pietro made sure that everyone was content to wait and would frequently offer them water from the well in the yard.

This gave him the chance to find out about the daily battles and whether he would need to close to avoid a skirmish that came too close to the mill. He was deathly afraid of these battles—not because of the bodily harm they might cause him, but for one single thing: fire. It would spell disaster. Mills had been known to burn so quickly and so hot that no one could do anything but stand and watch. Therefore, fire was the stuff of Pietro's nightmares. He would toss and turn in his bed so violently that he would land on the floor. Marta would lean over from her side of the bed and lay a comforting hand upon his back, reassuring him that it was only a dream.

But Pietro was only too aware that dreams can become reality, so he was as vigilant as a general in understanding the waves of troop movements and the outcomes of each battle for his business. The lives of his family depended on it.

∼

1515

Marta was late. She had slipped out the door early in the morning, hoping to find some grain and perhaps even a bit of lamb for the table. Perhaps some fish from the river. Pietro had slept through her departure but now paced anxiously, risking a look out of the window every few minutes. He could not chance leaving the house because outside a battle raged. They could hear it through the barricaded door—the men shouting, dying, the clash and clang as sword met sword, the occasional faint booming of the cannons. The soldiers would fight and then tire, fight and then tire. Periodically, they would quiet, as though exhausted by their own folly.

The Spaniards, the Germans, and the Venetians died outside of their door, for across the street was the Castello, which the Venetians were gallantly trying to defend. Andrea risked peeking out through a crack in the wall and Pietro grabbed him by his shirt and dragged him away from the front of the house, scolding him, and in a gesture driven by fear, gave him a whack on the backside. Andrea's cries echoed the deeper cries outside, but they were soon soothed away by Pietro, who stroked the boy's hair until he quieted.

After dark, when the battle had subsided, Pietro risked going out to look for Marta. He passed the still-warm bodies of the scarlet Spanish soldiers, their dark-haired heads bent at odd angles. The hefty Germans lay draped across stone and ground. The Venetian knights with their colored plumes resembled brightly colored birds struck down in mid-flight. Pietro brushed back a tear. He took the scarf from around his neck and pulled it over his nose, for the stink of death was already emanating from the bodies. Part of the horror of this war was that there were so many different factions causing confusion, uncertainty, and accidents. The "fog of war" was as common as the fog that rose from the Brenta River in the mornings.

It wasn't until the small hours of the morning started to reveal the monumental carnage that Pietro finally spied her. Her body was lying on the side of the road. Unlike most of the bodies that surrounded her, she was seemingly free of injury. She looked as though she were asleep. Her eyes were closed; her head tilted to the side. Pietro knelt down and swept her up in his arms. It was then that he could feel what killed her, for her bones were crushed. She must have been run down by something very heavy. Something had mown her down like a dog.

When Pietro brought her back home, Andrea did not cry. Instead, he crawled up on the bed next to her body and tenderly leaned his head next to hers. To lose your mother at the age of seven is a terrible thing. You are old enough to understand that something irrevocably terrible has happened, but too young to find ways to cope with it. Her untimely death would haunt Andrea throughout his life, cropping up at moments of doubt and sorrow.

Chapter Three

1519–1521: THE FIRST APPRENTICESHIP

Pietro made sure that his son was educated. By the time he was ten, he could read and write. Pietro also taught him how to add and subtract, and how to keep accounts, because there were, as he put it, always people who were prepared to put their thumb upon the scale.

One day, Vincenzo rode up to the mill on a black mule that he had just bought at the livestock auction. He dismounted and ran his hand along the animal's withers. He showed Pietro the mule's teeth.

"Fifteen years old. Not a day older," he said proudly. "Only ridden by an old man on Sundays." He clapped the animal on the rump and the mule turned around and bit him on the shoulder. Vincenzo yelped and jumped out of range of the mule's surly, eye-rolling head. "Well, they didn't tell me about that!" he said and rubbed his shoulder gingerly.

Pietro offered him a glass of wine, which Vincenzo gratefully drank in one gulp.

But he was here for another purpose. Andrea was now almost eleven. He had exhibited an uncanny gift for numbers and drawing, and seemed to have not only an excellent facility with concepts of shape and form, but also a talent with materials and was already able to coax out beautiful forms in the soapstone that Vincenzo kept at his studio. *The boy had a gift*, he thought, and he said as much to Pietro.

Pietro responded by drawing a line in the soft dirt with his toe. He had always imagined that Andrea would apprentice with him. He had seen himself growing old, wizened and stooped, with his young son, now a man, at his side, shouting at the hopper and making deals with the cloister's baker. It was as it should be. A son carried on his father's work.

Vincenzo sat down on a bench, rubbing his shoulder. He pushed his shirt aside and examined it. The mule's large spatulate teeth had not broken the skin, but left deep indentations in two neatly curved lines. Neither man said anything for a few minutes. Vincenzo wanted to give Pietro the space and time to consider what he was suggesting.

He looked at his new prized mule. It had transformed in front of his eyes from a friend to an enemy. The mule looked at him through thick brown eyelashes, bored. "What is a nip between friends?" he seemed to say. "Forget about it." But Vincenzo was not about to forget. He thought about selling the mule for meat and then realized he would take too much of a loss. He considered trying to take him back to the auction house. What a ruckus he would cause. He would rail and cry, and they would listen patiently and then turn their backs, for everyone knew that sales were final at the livestock auction. Let the buyer beware.

Pietro, meanwhile, had been thinking as well, but he had been thinking about his only son. Andrea was slender and quick at everything he did. He would make a fine miller. He would help his father until he died and then carry on in the family tradition. He would raise a family, raise a son who would in turn take the mill as his life's work, and the cycle would continue.

But Pietro knew that the stones that ground the wheat would hang heavily around his son's neck. Although Andrea tried to hide it, he only had eyes for stone that he could shape—not the stones of a mill.

His eyes would light up when he described his most recent trip to Vincenzo's. Pietro saw Andrea's hands enthusiastically scribing in the air, trying to show him how the rock was being shaped. He heard how much faster the boy would speak. Andrea continually brought back small artifacts from his day—a fossilized shell discovered in a chip of stone, the beginnings of a small marble wreath that he had been working on, the drawing of a whippet. He delivered these to his parents with pride, and the house filled with stone and paper, wood and chalk.

Vincenzo knew that Andrea could find himself a good living in stone masonry, for as he grew up, it became clear that Andrea had a facility with numbers, an appreciation of form, and he was not afraid of heavy or difficult work. He also sported a kind of honest charm which made him a favorite with his peers and with his elders.

Vincenzo introduced him to architectural drawings and one of the first buildings that Andrea became enamored with was the Basilica di San Lorenzo. Vincenzo showed him a piece of *pietra serena*, Italian dark stone, which was used as foundational material. He taught him about the concept of proportion—and had Andrea choose his favorites from a variety of drawings. They would discuss why one proportion seemed more pleasant than another, why architects chose certain materials over others, why this form followed this function.

Pietro and Vincenzo accompanied Andrea on his first day as apprentice with the stone cutter Bartolomeo Cavazza da Sossano. At eight in the morning the streets were already filled with people. It was Sunday, October 31, 1521. They were overtaken by a confraternity, a group of men dressed in flowing white robes, most carrying banners or crosses, some with red chasubles covering their shoulders. Andrea felt as though he had been overtaken by a flock of swans. He was reminded that he had not gone to church for many months. Perhaps some Sunday he and his father would go to Santa Sofia, the oldest church in the city. He enjoyed the ringing echoes of the choir and the chance to spend time leisurely looking up at the elegance of the soaring arches.

As they approached the stone cutter's studio, they heard a rough voice shouting. A few seconds later, a young man came flying out of the arched opening and landed sprawling in the dust before them. They helped him up and beat the dust from his clothing. Between coughs, he managed to gasp, "Signore Cavazza caught me using the wrong chisel."

Pietro, Vincenzo, and Andrea exchanged looks. This was not an auspicious start.

Cavazza met them at the door. His face was mostly lower jaw with a mouth that pulled the rest of his face downward. His eyes had the meanness of a pig; enveloped by extra flesh, they peered at Andrea as though he were a piece of slightly rotting veal. He smelled of spilled wine.

Pietro was tempted to take his son away, to save him from a man who was obviously callous and abusive. He squeezed Andrea's shoulder, telegraphing *Should we go?* But Andrea, only thirteen, had a stubborn spine that had always kept him upright in times of trouble. He shouldered the extra packet his father had carried for him and went into the stonemason's studio, thinking about the Christians going into the lion's den. Vincenzo gave him a few coins and a look that said *Let us know.*

Cavazza did not disappoint. He was as mean as his face. No matter the weather, each morning he woke his seven charges up with a ladle of cold water. Andrea's trick was to train himself to wake up when Cavazza came into the room. He would leap from his pallet a hair before Cavazza could start his day with shivers. It became a little game between them, and when

Cavazza succeeded in throwing water in Andrea's face, the stone cutter would smile, satisfied that he had inflicted yet another small injustice on one of his many apprentices.

Although Andrea was not a young man prone to hatred, he grew to hate Cavazza, for the man was a bully, a tyrant, and a sycophant, groveling around the wealthy like an obsequious duck.

The boy who had been booted out of the door became one of Andrea's best friends and they often manipulated their day of work so that they could be together. His name was Stefano and he had been born to a poor family in Rome. His mother had been forced to sell him to Cavazza when her husband had been lost to a wasting disease. Stefano still got teary when he spoke about that awful day when his mother had avoided his eyes and turned away from him without looking back.

Andrea's first job was to carry stones from the ox cart to the storage area, and since Stefano was often in trouble, he was usually working side by side with Andrea. Together they survived Cavazza's torturous ways and they both managed to graduate from simply carrying stones to carving them.

There was no denying the fact that Cavazza enjoyed causing tears to flow. He would often cuff the boys about the ears if they made mistakes and his punishment for a bad cut was to starve them for the day. As far as Andrea could tell, he never drank anything but wine and he was drunk most of the time.

As Andrea's hate for Cavazza grew, his love for the alabaster, marble, and granite that transformed into fantastic shapes under his hand grew as well. He might have stayed there forever if it hadn't been for an event that propelled him to try to escape.

Stefano died.

The dust from the stones had always made Stefano cough and his lungs wheezed and clanked like a badly built forge. He tried to wear a cloth around his mouth, but Cavazza rudely jerked it off his face when he saw it, claiming he needed to see their faces to "keep them honest."

Stefano developed a racking cough that tortured him through the night so that he never truly slept. Andrea attempted to wake Stefano up before Cavazza entered the shed that served as their room, but Cavazza would enter from the other door, wearing soft shoes, or enter before dawn and drown Stefano with freezing water. This only exacerbated Stefano's cough, and after a few weeks, he was unable to rise from his bed. In two days, he was dead.

Because he had lost his mother at such an early age, death was especially painful for Andrea. It resonated in his head and his heart, and when he realized that Stefano would never rise from his bed again, his loss turned immediately to fear. He would run.

He had seen what happened to boys who ran, for Cavazza had made friends with some members of the military, giving them free cornices with only minor flaws. These men brought the boys back and pocketed the finding money, and like Stefano's mother, never looked back.

Andrea knew that Cavazza beat every boy who ran, stopping only when they passed out or when his arm tired, but Andrea didn't care. He would leave, go back to his father's house, and begin his life again. Perhaps he would follow in his family's footsteps and become a miller. Or perhaps he could be like his uncle, a gondolier. Punting boats around a placid lake or a riling river would be preferable to this torture.

The night after Stefano's body was removed and presumably buried in a pauper's field, Andrea made his break. He waited until the snores of the boys reached that moment when all tension in their bodies had ceased and their breath had stretched and calmed. As he pushed the shutters open, they made only one small squeak of a sound. He leapt out of the window and began to run. He hadn't realized how oppressive the atmosphere had been in that cloudy, dust-filled environment, and as he ran, he began to shed the heaviness of the past year. He walked all night and fell asleep under a willow tree near the Bacchiglione River, listening to it whisper and sigh to him.

He was kicked awake by a boot. The boot belonged to one of Cavazza's military friends who yanked Andrea to his feet. He began to claw and punch in anger as though he could bring Stefano back with every blow. But he was no match for a military man of that size. The man clubbed him in the chin and lifted the dazed Andrea over his shoulder. Andrea's bloom of anger was doused by the blow. Andrea found himself dumped in the dirt in Cavazza's stone yard, and true to every rumor, Cavazza beat him until blood ran from his ears and he lost consciousness.

The next morning, Cavazza woke him with his customary cold water. Andrea stumbled painfully out of bed and to the stone yard. As he began to polish a fine piece of alabaster, his first thought was that he would kill Cavazza or be killed by him. He was certain that blood would be seen in the dust, and whether it was his or Cavazza's scarcely mattered to him. Cavazza swept by and ignored him, which made Andrea even angrier. He was swimming in his own anger, so caught up in planning revenge that it took several minutes for him to realize that someone was standing next to him. It was his father.

Pietro took one look at Andrea's swollen face and, without another word, picked him up—which was not difficult to do since Andrea had lost so much weight—and began to stride out of the yard.

Cavazza ran up to Pietro and grabbed him by the arm. "I have put money into this boy," he whined. "I have trained this boy. He is good for nothing, but I have tried my best with him and he has rewarded me by running away. You owe me money for all of the time I have trained this boy."

Pietro stared at Cavazza and said in a quiet, steely voice, "If you ever touch my boy again, I will kill you myself." And then he turned and walked away without looking back.

Andrea buried his face in his father's shoulder, smelling him, taking in his warmth. Once again, he was safe.

Chapter Four

1523: THE BIG MOVE

Pietro tightened the ropes that covered the canvas on their rented ox cart. Fifteen-year-old Andrea was busy cutting a rosebush switch that he could use on the stubborn oxen. The one nearest to him, the one with tan spots, craned his neck and stared at him as though he understood exactly what was in Andrea's mind.

It would take two days of travel. Both Andrea and Pietro were looking forward to it. It was time to leave Padua and its sad memories behind. They stopped off and put yellow roses on Marta's grave and then set off. Indeed, the tan-spotted ox was always a little behind his white companion, and Andrea found that he had to use the rosebush switch all the way to Vicenza.

The trip was a chance for Andrea and Pietro to enjoy each other. That night, after they had fed and watered the thin oxen, they sat by the fire and talked about everything from the sun to the moon, wars and peacetimes, and what made people act the way they did (God made them that way). Pietro told stories of Marta, her warmth, her ability to—as he put it—"make cakes out of two grains of wheat."

Andrea listened attentively. He leaned back and stared at the rotation of the heavens. He watched as the stars moved across the sky and marveled at their beauty.

Later that night while they were both staring up at the sky, Pietro told a story that had been told to him by his brother, Lucca, the gondolier. One bright night, a certain passenger beckoned to him from the pier, a man with a long face and a sheaf of dark hair that cut across his forehead. The man needed to be taken downriver from Vigodarzere to Cadoneghe, so it took quite some time. Lucca remembered it as a quiet evening free of wind or even moonlight, so the stars were staring down on them and they were bathed in starlight. The man was a little drunk and sipped wine as he talked. He said that he had been thinking about the heavens and how the heavens might not be spinning around the earth, but rather around the sun. He said this with a laugh, as if the thought were a kind of joke.

As Lucca docked and helped his odd passenger out of the boat, the passenger slipped and one foot disappeared into the mud. It took the two of them several minutes to recover the man's slipper, rinse it free of mud, and then return it to his foot. The man sat on the dock and laughed until he cried, saying something about the largeness of the heavens and the smallness of a shoe. He introduced himself as Nicolaus Copernicus, and Lucca had remembered the name, for the man and the night had been memorable all around.

Andrea thought about the idea—the heavens rotating around the sun—and decided that indeed the man had been drunk and creative with his thoughts. One could clearly see that the stars went from one horizon to the other, spinning around the earth as surely as God sat at the head of his Holy table. Still, it was refreshing to have to grapple with new ways of thinking; it stretched and exercised the mind, and Andrea enjoyed the heady feeling.

Soon after that, Pietro rolled over and started his customary heavy snoring. But Andrea stayed up, his arms behind his head, staring at the night sky. One could travel so far in one's own mind while hardly moving an inch.

When they neared Vicenza, Andrea marveled at the ancient Roman wall that surrounded the city. It was built out of brick and stone in a striation that was somehow both chaotic and planned. Greenery cascaded down parts of the walls and Andrea imagined it as trickles of green water. *How the Romans had labored over this wall,* he thought, seeing each brick and stone as a record of an effort from long ago. *Perhaps that is what buildings are: simply recordings of human effort and imagination.* He made his father stop the cart so that he could brush his hand over the wall, feeling its roughness and the way each brick had been placed.

For a moment, he was that mason, long ago just a pile of ash, and yet immortalized in this bit of wall, this stone, which was such a small part of such a large wall and yet so critical. For what is a wall without every stone? He laid his ear against the wall and listened, imagining that he could hear the voice of the long-ago mason as he sang an ancient song.

His father called to him and Andrea leapt back in the ox cart, eager to get on to his new life, for he had landed a new apprenticeship—hopefully with a kinder master and a more generous situation than the one he had left behind in Padua.

Andrea's first impression of Vicenza was of winding cobblestoned streets defined by rows of buildings that served a wide variety of purposes. Houses were side by side with churches, storefronts were capped by city palaces that were owned by the wealthy, and everyone walked the slender streets together. It was a city where the rich and the poor flowed through the narrow streets like amiable trout in a stream.

The central square, the Piazza dei Signori, however, was dominated by the Palazzo della Ragione, a large building that had seen better days. Crowned by a long domed turquoise roof, it must have been a beautiful edifice that the people of the city had been proud of. Now, it stank of neglect. Although a variety of shops were on the lower floor and people flowed in and out of them, the southwest corner had collapsed and ill-fitting scaffolding propped the walls up. Pietro clicked his tongue. What an eyesore. Andrea could not take his eyes off of the collapsed corner. It was like looking at a gaping wound. They turned away from this sad sight.

The next day they were able to rent a small apartment on the second floor near the square on a lovely little street called Stradella dell'Isola. But they would often pass through the Piazza dei Signori and the neglected Palazzo della Ragione continued to bother them both like an itch that they could not scratch.

Chapter Five

1524: ADMITTED TO THE GUILD

Giovanni was indeed as unlike Cavazza as a horse is unlike a pig. He was an exceedingly slender man, and tall, and when he loomed over Andrea's work and carefully repositioned Andrea's grip on his rasp, it was as though Andrea were in the shadow of God himself. Giovanni was kind and careful and slow, with a kind of plodding deliberation that seemed right for the working of stone. He was one half of the partnership of Giovanni di Giacomo da Porlezza and Girolamo Pittoni, two men who ran a cheerful, respected stone masonry and architectural design shop.

Although Giovanni was the botegga's architect, he was also the man who spent a lot of his time in the yard, carefully watching the nine apprentices as they made mistakes and learned from those mistakes—or didn't. He was patient with a kind of fatherly approach to each boy. He understood the concept of rewards and frequently brought in *cannoli de crema* or *chocolatti* even though they were usually reserved for the time of Carnevale. Perhaps that was because he was married to Anna, a baker of some local reputation, who enjoyed giving pleasure to everyone in the form of sugary treats. Punishment was not laid out in terms of physical pain, but rather in being given less and less responsibility. This was an effective kind of psychic torture, for in this environment, everyone wanted to succeed.

Andrea was the kind of apprentice that everyone wanted—bright, capable, watchful, tenacious, and good with his hands. He seemed to have an innate understanding of materials. He understood that one needed a certain brutality around granite, a kind of tenderness around sandstone, and a way to caress and polish marble. He was a pleasure to work with and he made friends easily with the other boys, the clients, and his masters.

Giovanni began to take a special interest in Andrea, recognizing that the boy was made up of materials that were almost as strong as the materials he worked with. Andrea soon graduated from rough cuts to intricate carving. He had a special love for rosettes, which reminded him of his mother, who used to bring home yellow roses even in the face of war.

Giovanni began to include Andrea during his conversations with potential clients. These clients ranged from simple shopkeepers who needed a retaining wall to contain the cows to priests who wanted a new facade on their church to wealthy landowners who were interested in a new house in the country. He tasked Andrea with mathematical problems, with issues of stress and mass and pitch.

Giovanni's partner, Girolamo Pittoni, also became fond of

Andrea. Girolamo was the sculptor of the house, carefully tending his stones as though tending a garden. The stones seemed to grow under his care. Each day, they transformed slowly from a block to a subtle shape to a definitive form—a flower, a face, a hand, a coin.

For Andrea, it was a kind of magic. Girolamo never hurried, never cursed, never struck the stone in anger, for he knew that to strike a stone in anger was to potentially lose the stone forever. The stone was unforgiving and would break under assault, but thrive given care and kindness. Girolamo and Giovanni treated their boys like their stones, and both the stones and the boys blossomed.

Andrea was enjoying the fruits of Somnus, the Roman god of sleep. He was rolling down a hill on a sunlit mountainside, for some reason protecting a small lamb, when the sound of banging interrupted his freefall. He bolted awake.

Girolamo poked his head into Andrea's attic room and said, "Sleepyhead! Time to go!" and then his head disappeared.

Andrea responded by leaping into his clothes. This was not usual and he was curious to find out where they were going.

Girolamo hefted his girth onto a large cart drawn by two muscled oxen. He headed south, out the gates toward the Berici Hills. They were going to get stone.

Andrea knew about these hills only from the stone they provided. He knew about Vicenza sandstone, for example, a mellow white stone with speckles of green and brown that hardened with time. It had proven the perfect material to carve—for stone, it was relatively easy. Occasionally, when he was chiseling a curl or curve, he would run into a small fossilized creature. Sometimes they resembled the small gray pill bugs that he found on the forest floor and sometimes more like a seashell. These small imperfections only endeared the stone to Andrea more completely, for he embraced the imperfections of nature as one of God's designs.

As they rolled along, Girolamo whistled snatches of folk songs, comic *frottola*, madrigals. Andrea sat back and watched as black and white starlings swooped and darted and pale doves fled away from the muffled jowls of the oxen. The day was sparkling—white, gold, green, and blue. For a moment, Andrea wished that he were a painter. The colors and light were so harmonic that the scene seemed embedded within his eye.

As they rode down the Berica River road, they passed through the villages of Villaga and Lumignano. They could already see the limestone cliffs, looming on the horizon like an ominous bank of clouds. As they threaded their way into those cliffs, the oxen groaned, complaining about the steepness of the road and the weight of their empty cart.

Girolamo switched them lightly and laughed. "Wait until you feel this cart all loaded with stone! Then, my fine beasts, you will have something to complain about!"

They finally stopped in a small valley that was ringed on three sides by mountain slopes. Three men were waiting for them, sitting amid a plentiful pile of varietal stones. They had built a block and tackle apparatus that would assist them in hefting the stones into the cart. Andrea and Girolamo looked at each stone, examining them for cracks, fissures, and weaknesses.

Some of the stone was Nanto stone, which was highly prized for its gold hue. They chose carefully, recognizing that the oxen could handle only a small fraction of the stones available. After Girolamo had solidified the deal, the men began to load the wagon. Girolamo stayed to watch but encouraged Andrea to explore the hillsides, understanding that young men needed to be kept on long leashes.

Andrea climbed into the hills, breathing the fresh mountain air. It felt thinner, cleaner than the Vicenzan air, but imagination running wild can make even the air change. He spied a large hole in the side of the hill and decided to head for it. He climbed with a will, occasionally stopping to drink from his flask of water. He finally pulled himself up and over the last yellow rock (noting that it was of Nanto stone) and found himself in a clearing, staring into the mouth of a cave. This cave glared at him from the calcified stone cliffs. He hesitated for a moment, thinking about demons and other evil creatures, but then he stopped and took the temperature of the day. It was bright and warm, and the sensibility of the place was one of God, not one of the devil. He went in.

The coolness felt good on his sweaty brow and it took a moment for him to get used to the dark. He turned back toward the entrance and realized that people had lived there long ago, for the entrance was supported by brickwork. Without realizing it, he had entered through an archway. Other brick openings acted as windows. He examined the wall closely. A kind of mortar had been used to build the wall, and Andrea imagined people from long ago, dancing the same dance that the masons performed when building the walls for Vicenza.

He wandered further into the cave. There was evidence of fires—in one area the ceiling was black with soot, and on the floor was a crude fireplace. Nothing extra had been done to the walls, which formed a graceful curve that would allow comfortable leaning. He sat down and tried it himself and found that the walls supported his back and his head. *No wonder they had made no changes*, he thought. He sat there for a moment, enjoying the coolness, the silence, and then reluctantly stood up. *He could live here*, he thought, and began to analyze why he felt that way.

There was plenty of beautiful light; plenty of air; a satisfying and beautiful curve to the walls that also proved useful to the human body. He was musing about water, wondering how difficult it would be to bring water up from the valley below when he realized he could hear water dripping further back in the cave. He followed the sound a few more lengths in and found a natural shallow bowl, slimy with a thousand years of water. There was the final piece: a perfect place to raise a family, for they could see the enemy approach and they had a reliable water source.

He trundled down the mountain to find the stones loaded. Girolamo was just paying the men off when Andrea approached, the mystical air of the mountain cave still wrapped around him. Girolamo looked at him with curiosity but said nothing. Andrea clambered onto the cart and they set off without another word.

Andrea's mind was not on the scenery that slowly changed as

they made their way ponderously down the mountain. Instead, it was still in the cave home that had been so beautifully rendered. Water, air, views, comfort, light. All this time spent in the wonders of religious monuments had not driven home an essential thought, but the little cave home had. Architecture could change the soul. He had felt his heart opening, his pulse slowing, his mind calming. He now knew that a building was not just a place to take shelter from the rain, but also a place that could shape a life.

Andrea was on his knees and covered with the dust of the limestone pillar he was attempting to carve. He had been working in the studio for months now, a place of so much banging and shouting that he often shoved rags in his ears. Because of this, he did not immediately hear when Girolamo charged into the room. He was an enormous man who led with his bulbous head, and for such a large man, he moved fast and was next to Andrea's side before Andrea even realized it.

Andrea looked up. He saw that Girolamo was shouting something. He held a rolled paper with a red ribbon and kept raising that arm as though in victory. Andrea took the rags from his ears and heard the tumult of the banging in the yard and Girolamo shouting, and it finally dawned on him what his mentor was saying.

"Andrea! Andrea! You have been admitted into the guild!"

Such a moment. This meant he had maintained the status of a journeyman. He could now travel and learn from other members of the guild. He would be a respected man who knew his craft, a man who could be relied upon for good workmanship and a high level of skill. This meant everything changed, for he was now official. A professional. At sixteen years old, he had already established that he knew a little something.

That night he and his friends celebrated with wine, some of Anna's cannoli, and sweet layers of tiramisu.

Both Girolamo and Giovanni now began to treat Andrea differently, as he had proven himself worthy of their energy. The morning after Andrea received his document, Giovanni led him into a room he had never seen before and sat him down at a large desk. Andrea looked around him. The room was stocked with flat drawers that were especially designed for drawings and plans and the walls were covered in so many drawings that they were an inch thick.

Giovanni opened the drawer with caution and took out a large piece of parchment. He laid it out carefully in front of Andrea. It featured a series of elevations and was labeled "On Perspective." The drawing was by Sebastiano Serlio and contained three theatrical scenes: a tragedy, a comedy, and a satire. Each one featured a series of lines that culminated in a single point. The streets, the eaves of the buildings, and each detail from the steps to the crenulations above the windows followed those lines and ended there. When Giovanni asked him where the lines intersected, Andrea was clear and laid his pen upon the single spot. Giovanni sat down to talk more about perspective and how the human eye sees.

From that day forward, a large part of his day consisted of

looking at drawings and then copying them. This was slow work, but it forced him to pay attention to the smallest of details. Every line and circle and indeed every dot was a critical part of the drawing, and without that feature, the result would be a different building.

Andrea found that he had a facility for details. He enjoyed drawing individual elements such as patera (small decorative dish shapes) and guilloche (little drop-like ornaments). He pored over works by Giulio Romano, Porlezza, Falconetto, and Sanmicheli, for this was the way that young architects learned.

One day, Giovanni brought out a large tome that had been gathering dust on top of a cabinet. It was Vitruvius's *De Architectura* ("Of Architecture"). Andrea sat down to have a look.

Hours later, Giovanni tapped him on the shoulder. Andrea looked up, surprised to find that the day had seeped out from under him and that it was evening. He had lost himself in the construction of waterwheels, aqueducts, public baths, and water clocks; at the use of plumb lines, pulleys, and catapults.

Vitruvius had pulled together a wide variety of topics under the umbrella of architecture: pumps and central heating; an investigation into materials such as stucco, brick, and lime; subjects such as steam engines, town planning, pavement, and temples. There seemed to be nothing that did not touch architecture. This broad way of thinking resonated with Andrea, for he, too, saw the interconnectivity in these things.

Some of Vitruvius's ideas about architecture revolved around the human form and he used it as a kind of caliper that could describe the perfect proportion—from side to side, the body (and the building) should be symmetrical, but from back to front, it could be asymmetrical. The perfect human body was a series of related measurements: a palm was equal to four fingers, a foot was equal to four palms, a cubit was six palms, four cubits made a man, a pace was four cubits, a man was twenty-four palms. Andrea looked at his own palms and determined that, indeed, his palm was about four of his fingers across. This elementary and illuminating way of looking at something that he had used to peel potatoes pleased him no end.

Vitruvius's theory about how to design buildings was simple: *utilitas, firmitas,* and *venustas* (useful, sturdy, and delightful). As Andrea strolled home that night it became a kind of tune: *utilitas, firmitas, and venustas . . . utilitas, firmitas, and venustas.* He whistled it all the way to bed.

Chapter Six

1525: NOW AN ORPHAN

Andrea had no more tears. The priest had given his father his last rites. There was nothing left to be said. Andrea sat next to his father's bed and sponged his hot brow. Pietro's cough had grown worse over the hours Andrea had been sitting there, but now, he was quiet. Andrea put his hand on his father's chest; yes, he was still breathing, although it was shallow and rapid.

Pietro had made certain that his son could always see a path forward. He ensured that Andrea was connected to the right people and that he knew how to observe and copy the correct speech and behavior. These were important talents, for Pietro knew that Andrea would have to surmount the obstacle of being from the working class. He would not have any advantages of birth, but would have to make a name for himself through sheer talent, ambition, and skill.

Andrea dragged himself to his desk and sat down. He stared

at the drawings from only last week—when life had seemed like a well-oiled axle, rolling along without noise or friction.

During these times, when death became a part of life and the veils of existence were transparent, Andrea was filled with overwhelming questions. They seemed to overflow, pouring from his mind like water from a pitcher. He knew that he should have the answers, for the priest had provided him with them, but there were these times, when he saw people in pain, that he could not reconcile his image of God with the presence of unnecessary suffering. Why did his father have to suffer if God was the architect of all things? He, who had power over all, could create an existence that was filled with beauty and music, a life that was free of pain and violence. Instead, people suffered, fought, and died, unremarkable and unloved.

He looked up. Something had changed. He swiveled and looked at his father, lying in his bed. Andrea crossed the room, already knowing. His father was no longer on this earth. He took his father's mottled hand, the blood receded, the hand clammy, slick with the sweat of death, and he knew that life had indeed fled. Perhaps Pietro was already with his wife, Marta, a woman who no longer limped, but was young, carefree, and capable of dancing.

Andrea allowed himself to dissolve in grief. Pietro had been the father that any boy would have longed for. When Andrea was young, Pietro would wrestle with him, turning him upside down on his shoulder until Andrea squealed with laughter and the blood rushed into his ears. He was a father who had supported him, loved him, and protected him.

When Andrea could cry no more, he squared his shoulders and washed his face in the nearby basin. He would do everything he could to make his father and his mother proud. They would look down from the kingdom of heaven and rejoice, for their son was a moral man, a skilled artisan, a good father, and a good husband. He would use all the gifts that his parents and God had given him. He would make the world a better place, a more beautiful existence.

Andrea sat in the square admiring three pigeons. He had a fondness for them. Their strutting, bobbing heads reminded him of some men he knew who strutted and fluttered their way down the streets. These three—two females and a male—were engaged in a classic love triangle, but it was clear who was going to win this battle of romance. The male was puffed up, looking twice his normal size. He followed an iridescent female, and as she bobbed her head horizontally, her beak leading her body, the male mimicked her. Bop, bop, bop. The third bird followed a respectable distance behind, already understanding that she was out of this race. The first two careened around the cobblestones, flirting and flying, he pursuing and she escaping, her beak in the air. Then, when he seemed to have lost interest, she flew near him, fanning his fires. He responded by dragging his tail feathers on the cobblestones. Finally, they were in sync. They grabbed each other by the beak as though exchanging food and cooed at each other.

Andrea reflected on this. He needed a wife.

Chapter Seven

1534: LOVE AND MARRIAGE

Andrea was exactly twenty-six years old and his birthday party was in full swing. A baker had made him a moon-shaped cake, an homage to the Greeks, who were in turn paying tribute to Artemis, goddess of the moon. Andrea now put candles on it just like the Greeks had done. As he lit them, his friends oohed and laughed; they had already enjoyed several bottles of wine. Andrea, too, was in a fine mood for he had seen his wife-to-be.

He had noticed her working in a carpenter's shop only that morning. Hearing that a new and highly skilled carpenter had moved to town, Giovanni had dispatched him to the shop. Andrea walked in and immediately saw a young woman sitting at a table, poring over sheets of paper filled with numbers. She was a beauty with black hair that foamed down her back and a face filled with large brown eyes that looked up and met his when he entered. She did not look away. He found himself having to break her gaze by looking at his boots.

A boy had taken him to the famed carpenter's workbench and she had watched with a kind of covert attitude of disapproval that Andrea couldn't understand. Did she not like him? The boy led him to the carpenter, whose name was gaining much recognition, but within a half hour of seeing the man's work, Andrea found corruption instead of competence. As he asked for examples of the man's skills and interrogated him about his techniques, it became clear that the man claiming brilliance was instead stealing someone else's. Andrea quickly discovered the subterfuge and found the man who was the truly skilled carpenter sitting in a darker and less prestigious corner. He had been watching from the sideline, wondering if his skills were to be stolen yet again.

As this small drama unfolded, the woman with the dark hair stood in the back of the room and watched Andrea with her arms crossed. He could feel her eyes following him, taking in the situation and carefully evaluating him. This woman was no fool. She watched as Andrea contracted the man in the corner to work with him. When the man smiled in appreciation, Andrea clapped him on the back and shook his hand. *An architect was only as good as his workmen*, he thought, and told the man as much.

As Andrea left, the woman was also leaving. She opened the door and looked at him, saying only "*È una bella giornata.*"

Could he read anything special in those five words: "It is a beautiful day"? He could. He did.

It was not until later than he learned her name: Allegra-donna.

Their courtship was relatively simple since Allegradonna was an orphan. Both of her parents had perished in one of the long arms of a plague year. She had been ten years old at the time, and fortunately for her, the Lady Poiana, one of Vicenza's elite, had taken her in as a maid. Allegradonna was immediately perceived as more than maid material, however, for she had a superior way with numbers and taught herself to read within a year. She quickly rose through the ranks to become Lady Poiana's close confidant. Lady Poiana allowed her to do sums for other businesses to make extra money, which is where Andrea had found her.

Under the watchful eyes of Lady Poiana's mother-in-law, her dead husband's irascible mother, Allegradonna and Andrea entertained themselves by playing with numbers, as they both had a rich love of them. They were both enamored with mathematical games based on ratios. Andrea favored comparing 3:4 to 2:3 and he would make whimsical drawings for her of fantastical buildings made of squares, circles, and triangles embellished with trees, leaves, and lions.

They also shared a love of drawing, a love of shapes. Once, while they were courting, they had a picnic down by the Brenta. Lady Poiana had assigned a giggly chambermaid to accompany them. She sat down by the river, her shoes off, her feet dangling in the icy water, which left Andrea and Allegradonna free to hold hands while they sat on a rush mat.

"Your nails are the color of rose blossoms," said Andrea as he held her hand in his.

Allegradonna smiled, examined his hands, and shot back, "Your nails are the color of dead fish eyes!"

Many young men would have been shocked at this comment, but he thought about it seriously for they also shared a love of color. They talked for another hour on what color his nails actually were and concluded that it was a matter of how fresh the fish was. Fresh fish have a clear eye. With shared laughter they decided his nails were more in line with those of fish that were at least three days old. Certainly, they reflected a ground-in whiteness due to his many hours dealing with stone. After they had exhausted this topic, Allegradonna raised his hand to her lips and kissed it.

"Your nails are the color of old fish eyes, but your hand is that of an artist," she said and smiled at him in her direct way.

Allegradonna was as tart as a lemon. She had a spicy sense of humor and a mind that was so fast it was usually two steps ahead of Andrea's own. She was perfect for him and Andrea finally knew what it was like to love deeply and without a doubt.

When they married, Allegradonna brought with her a quilt decorated with birds of paradise and palm fronds, some sheets she had sewn, and a simple wooden bed of oak, all courtesy of Lady Poiana. Andrea was happier than he had ever been in his life, for he had found a woman who was a rare character, a woman who spoke her mind and was as funny as she was wry. It did not hurt that she was also smart—the daughter of a carpenter who could help him in his business and a woman who understood the beauty inherent in numbers.

They settled into a small rented house with a large room

upstairs that could serve as both their bedroom and his studio. It was not far from Giacomo da Porlezza and Girolamo Pittoni's workshop so Palladio could walk home for lunch and spend the *riposo*, the hot hours of the afternoon, with his new love.

Life for Palladio now took on a certain harmony. His life was a sweet litany of home cooked tagliatelle and spirited debates after the fine meal about life, love, and art. His work was a series of challenges that he could rise to with determination and will, for he loved working for both Giacomo and Girolamo. They challenged him every day, and when they saw that he could draw almost anything with imagination as well as accuracy, and that he had a gift for being personable, popular, and pleasant, they began to rely on him to meet with prestigious clients.

Chapter Eight

1537: ANDREA MEETS TRISSINO

Gian Giorgio Trissino was one of the most influential people in Vicenza. Andrea had expected to meet with him for only a few minutes. They would discuss the shape and form of the columns that Trissino had ordered for the entrance to his gardens, and then Andrea would be led out and would go back to work. He was a little nervous about this meeting, but he was also curious, for Trissino was rumored to be that rare man who combined wealth with fairness, culture with creativity. He was known to measure a man not by his family and the implied wealth or poverty, but by the actions and words of the man himself.

Andrea was there until the next morning. They had discussed all matters of the world all night: poetry, aesthetics, math, linguistics, philosophy, war and then peace. The conversation was like a thread unraveling—one thing led to another and there seemed no end to it. When they discovered that they were both ardent devotees of Vitruvius, the author, architect, and engineer who had lived in ancient Rome and written the work *De Architectura*, the conversation became, if possible, even more animated.

It happened well after midnight. The stars and the full moon stared down at them and the multiple candles that Trissino had long ago called for lit the garden with pools of light.

"You know of Vitruvius?" Trissino leaned in and almost set his beard on fire with the nearby candle.

"I believe that Vitruvius was a genius," replied Andrea, a bit tentative at first. Who was he to talk as an equal with this great man? But clearly Trissino did not see a miller's son—he saw something else.

Andrea appreciated the fact that Trissino would take the time to talk to a young man who, although clever and somewhat educated, was still from a lower class. But he treated Andrea as though he had something to contribute and for that, Andrea was grateful.

Due to the silver that streaked Trissino's abundant red beard, Andrea assumed that he was in his early sixties. He had a quiet way about him that Andrea found calming, but when he became excited about an idea, he would usually stand and pace as though the ideas would not sit still inside him, so he, in turn, could not sit still either.

As Andrea watched him, he thought he also saw great sadness in him. When Trissino was not actively engaged in thinking, Andrea felt he could see tragedy in those intelligent eyes. But this whiff of sadness would only be seen in brief and covered glimpses, between the pouring of more wine or the outpouring of new ideas.

Both Andrea and Trissino had studied Vitruvius not only as an architect, but also as a military engineer. They marveled in his ability to set up what they considered a functioning military city, for everything had to be taken into consideration: the approach and safety of the camp, hospital, mess hall, bathhouses, water, and latrines.

When they had finished analyzing his military abilities, they went on to discuss his ideas about the human body, proportion, and beauty. They laughed over the navel, the center of the body and yet a small space that not only determined the center of the universe, but was also somehow a comical spot. How fitting, they howled, for it was now approaching dawn, that the center of the universe was a small dent in the middle of one's stomach whose form varied as much as buttons.

As Andrea left Trissino's house in the chill hours of dawn, a thought was sitting solidly in his mind. If it weren't for the fact that Vitruvius had written his books on architecture, his name would be lost to the vagaries of time. Andrea salted that thought away, but it was never far from his mind from that day forward.

Andrea was afraid. As he held Allegradonna's hand, he looked into her eyes and saw fear radiating like heat. She was about to give birth to their first child. He turned away briefly and consciously pushed his own fear aside. When he turned back to her, he looked at ease, as though they were going on their first picnic. He stroked her brow and then left the women to do their work.

He plopped down in the nearest chair outside the room. As a father, he would need to make more money, and he wondered how that would be possible given his role at the workshop.

He was going to be a father. He thought now back to his own childhood—how his father had supported him, how he had intuited the challenges that were ahead of Andrea and did his best to prepare him. He had understood from the beginning that Andrea's road would be uphill due to the circumstances of his birth.

What could Andrea do for his son? Could he be as good a father as his own had been? Would his son grow up to be a lawyer? An artist? Or, ironically, a miller?

And what would he do if the baby was a girl? This new thought brought a special twinge of fear, for baby girls were, in his mind, like delicate panes of glass.

But when he took his squalling new son, Leonida, into his arms, his worries and fears faded away like dust. He kissed the black-haired boy and smelled a newborn, fresh as hay. His son. A beautiful creation. Allegradonna smiled—tired, happy, and complete.

One memorable sunny afternoon in July 1538, Trissino

summoned Andrea to his palazzo. He was ushered into the central courtyard, which was alive with bees and butterflies flitting in and out of the shadows made by the two stone pines that provided most of the shade. Two men sat at the table. They were younger than Andrea, but clearly possessed of wealth and power, with the air of men who were born in silk. Trissino introduced them. The slighter of the two, with dark hair and dark eyes, was Daniele Barbaro. The larger-built man with almond-shaped eyes was Marcantonio, Daniele's younger brother. Three dogs sat at his feet under the table.

Andrea's entrance had interrupted their conversation, and after he was introduced and sat down, they began it again.

Daniele was in the middle of a point about perfection. "Aristotle was correct!" he roared, pounding his fist on the table for emphasis. "Perfect means complete. Complete!"

Marcantonio took an enormous gulp of wine and shot back as though firing a cannon. "Aristotle was an imbecile! Empedocles understood that perfection is in incompleteness! Now *there* is a man to study, not that simpering toady."

Daniele fired another salvo. "I am not sure that it even exists. It is a state that is ever out of reach. A domain of God." He looked up toward heaven as though asking for holy support.

Trissino enjoyed this back-and-forth between the brothers. "Andrea," he asked, "Do you know of an example of perfection?"

Andrea paused as all three men looked expectantly at him. The bees droned heavily around them. The butterflies silently distracted his thoughts as he struggled with the question.

Daniele swallowed a few grapes, which he washed down with chianti. Marcantonio reached down and fondled the spotted dog nearest his hand.

At last Andrea tactfully replied, "Perfection is something to reach for, although I am not certain it can be reached."

The men, appreciating this young man's careful and precise answer, all laughed in agreement.

Andrea paused and then spoke again, drawing his finger along the seam of the table. "Perhaps perfection is my son."

The men nodded, since they all knew that he had recently received a gift from God. A son whose sunny disposition, perfect head of black hair, and sinless existence was a kind of perfection.

Trissino proposed a toast to Andrea's son, proclaiming, "As close to perfection as *The Assumption of the Virgin*."

When Andrea looked at him quizzically, Trissino explained that it was a painting by Tiziano Vecelli on the high altar of the Basilica di Santa Maria Gloriosa dei Frari in Venice. The three men then launched into a spirited debate about size and scale, for the painting featured human figures that were larger than life so as to be seen by even the last row of the congregation.

Andrea listened. He had never been to Venice, which was only a few days' ride away. *Someday*, he thought.

It was clear that Trissino and the Barbaro brothers were old friends. They discussed topics that spanned politics, aesthetics, economics, and poetry. They were in that safe place of fellowship where they could disagree, pound the table, and remain the closest of friends. Perhaps even closer because of that secure knowledge of respect and honor. And Andrea, due to the past year of scholarship, was able to join in the conversation at various points.

When Vitruvius came up, the courtyard rang with their voices, for he was a hero they could all easily claim. The subject of proportions was not far behind.

After several more glasses of wine, the four men experimented actively with the concept of the human body.

Marcantonio, red in the face from wine, jumped up. "I volunteer to be Vitruvian man!" he exclaimed, and stood under one of the stone pines, arms outstretched.

Trissino asked the servants to bring various measuring tools and they proceeded to measure Marcantonio from head to toe. He made a patient model and only requested that they continue to ply him with wine and an occasional purple grape so that he could keep his arms and his spirits up.

After a while, of course, they realized that they could allow Marcantonio to lie on the ground. He collapsed like a man made of lead and took up a more comfortable position while they painstakingly pursued their measurements. After an hour, they proclaimed that Marcantonio was "perfection," for if they used his navel as the center, they could draw a circle that would touch his fingers as well as his toes. In addition, they tested the Vitruvian idea that if one measured a man from the head to the toe and then across the chest from one outstretched arm to the other, one would form a square. However, in their explorations, they realized that collectively the square's center was not the navel, but a point further down on the body.

This led to a discussion about proportion and Leonardo da

Vinci, an artist, engineer, and scientist who, with his drawings of the human body based on Vitruvius's ideas, had laid out a complete definition of it. Andrea contributed his own knowledge about the way that the body could be measured.

Daniele added, "Do you know that da Vinci wrote it all backwards so that it could only be seen correctly as a reflection?"

For once Trissino was surprised by a new bit of knowledge. "Well, why on earth would he do that? What was the significance of that?"

Marcantonio, dangling a carrot in his long fingers, said, "Perhaps it was a manipulation, a trick to make people pay attention to what they read."

Daniele disagreed. "Da Vinci wanted to add a level of mystery to his work. After all," he added thoughtfully, "Vitruvius was the one who had done most of the original thinking."

Andrea chimed in. "Perhaps it was just a matter of convenience." His companions stared expectantly at him as he continued, "Everyone who is left-handed has experienced the unfortunate fate of the hand smudging the ink as it passes over newly written words. Writing in reverse would prevent that problem."

Everyone laughed and congratulated him on this thought, for it was new to all of them.

Soon, Marcantonio was nodding off. Daniele—with the mischievousness known only to siblings—bade all the dogs, who had been enjoying their own torpor in the sullen laziness of the afternoon, to now rise and lick the cheeks of their master. With a roar, Marcantonio leapt to his feet, swaying slightly as he did so.

The afternoon was proclaimed a success, and the four friends—for Andrea was now counted as such—departed for their own homes to enjoy what was left of the afternoon.

Chapter Nine

1539: A NEW NAME

As they dined on figs and mozzarella, Trissino regarded his young friend, Andrea, as though seeing him from afar. It is a tragedy when one's own son does not match up to expectations, he was thinking. Trissino's first son, Guilio, was a bully. There was no other way to state it. Born of Trissino's first wife, beloved Giovanna, Guilio had always been the boy who lived his life sniffing out weaknesses in others. It did not help matters when Giovanna died suddenly of a high fever as Guilio was turning twelve. Losing the softening influence of his mother at that difficult age only solidified his rocky heart, and when Trissino fell in love again, this time to lovely Bianca Cornedo, Guilio's heart soured and turned black.

Although Guilio knew enough to feign a religious life, he thought that the Catholic doctrine was spineless and a waste of time. However, this did not stop him from becoming a high-level priest at the Vicenza cathedral. This position gave him the power he needed to wreak vengeance on his own family.

While Trissino was away in Venice, Guilio, backed by ten hired strongmen, had stormed into the Cornedo home. Bianca had been in the garden, gathering a fresh bouquet of roses, when she heard boots upon the marble floors. She stood, allowing them to fall to the grass, and waited. She was not surprised when Guilio burst from the house and demanded that all rights to her family's house were now his.

Bianca was indeed an engaging woman—slender, pale, and an appreciator of all things beautiful—but she was not strong. The birth of her single son, Ciro, had almost killed her. So the brutality of her stepson hit her like a physical blow. She could hear the screams of the servants and the breaking of furniture within the house, and those sounds left her so weak she collapsed to the ground, her face among the roses. Bianca never recovered; she died within a year.

Trissino shook himself out of his reverie. To compare his son with Andrea was to compare a rat with a lion. He regarded the young man who sat in front of him. He knew that Andrea was special. If all went well, he would become someone whose name would echo down the halls of history. He would need a new name. A name that would be unique. One that would propel him, as surely as an oar propels a punt, into new financial and social circles.

He put this idea to Andrea gently, knowing how much he had loved his father and mother. At first, Andrea was taken aback. A new name? It seemed to dishonor his family. But Trissino pressed on. Andrea di Pietro della Gondola—the name was that of a gondolier, not an artist, not a philosopher. A name could make the difference between success and failure. He needed a single name. Something that was memorable.

Andrea sat in his chair and rubbed the worn oak arm, deep in thought. He knew that his father had worried about his son's lineage. It mattered which class you were born into and his name solidly linked him with the lower classes. What would his father and mother want? He knew the answer.

He turned to Trissino and asked, "What name would you suggest?"

In truth, Trissino had been contemplating this question for weeks. He felt that Andrea was a rare young man. Gifted with a hungry mind and a creative approach to problem solving, he was also calm, humorous, and a delight to have at any table.

"I am reminded of Pallas Athena, the Greek goddess of wisdom and war," Trissino replied. "She was known for her calm demeanor. Something which you share. Even in the face of war, she was reluctant to fight without extenuating circumstances."

Andrea turned this over in his mind.

"I am also thinking about the day we met," Trissino said, "surrounded as we were by the sights and sounds of nature. Do you know of Palladius of Antioch?" When Andrea shook his head, he continued, "He was a hermit who had been canonized as a saint. He was known for living in the desert, content to enjoy it until a merchant was murdered near his cave. When the townspeople accused Palladius of the murder, he prayed and the dead man rose and defended him. He was not only a man who loved nature—he was also a man known for working wonders."

Andrea smiled. "Well, I hope that you do not think I will be able to raise the dead!"

Trissino laughed. "No. If you could, you already would have done it." A cloud of sorrow passed by his eyes. "I think that the name Palladio would suit you. What do you think?"

Andrea popped another grape in his mouth, chewing it slowly. *Palladio.* He nodded.

Trissino put his hand on Andrea's shoulder, knowing that this was a kind of turning point. Palladio. That would be the young man's name from now on.

That night, after having spent most of the evening out, Andrea greeted Allegradonna in the small room that served as a combination dining room and living room. She had stoked the fire, using valuable wood to do so, and waited up for him. She sat him down by the fire, took his coat and shoes off, and then laid into him as though she was impaling meat.

Allegradonna did not scream or cry. Instead, she asked him pointed questions and each one hit him like an arrow: "Why do you leave me at home alone every night? Why do you desert me with our new son? Don't you love me anymore?"

He stood up and crossed the room, picking up a large bag he had left at the door. He started bringing out food. A ham. Bread. Cheese. A half-eaten chicken. Grapes. Olives. He placed them on the table in front of Allegradonna as an offering.

"I do these things because I love you more than the sky

itself," he said, and took her in his arms. "Trissino has given me a new name. Palladio."

He watched her closely. A name, as everyone knew, was critical to fame. And Andrea wanted fame. Perhaps it was because he had not been born into a higher class. Perhaps it was just an impulse born of hubris. Or perhaps he simply feared disappearing as most people did, in death.

She stared at his face in the firelight and saw the question and the shy eagerness behind the question. What did she think?

She looked at him, scanning him from the tip of his head to the tips of his shoes. Here was a man she loved dearly. He was kind, smart, and treated her well, much better than most. She knew that he loved her. But a new name was something that took some thinking. For if he had a new name, so did she.

But she also saw something else in him. He was driven. He would strive toward what he wanted with his heart, and mind, and soul. And she knew what that meant. It meant that she would be alone much more often than if he were a simple gondolier or a shopkeeper or a herder. It would probably mean hardship, for to have such a lofty name was not only a kind of honor, but also a pressure, a burden.

She took his hand and softly put it to her cheek. "Mr. Palladio, can I still call you Husband?"

He kissed her in reply.

"I will still be angry sometimes when you come crawling home at dawn," she said. "And if you leave me for too long without a word, I will send the dogs after you. But know this, *Palladio*, I will do my best to help you. And perhaps someday, I will get my own kitchen in return." Then she grabbed a wooden spoon and pretended to threaten him with it. They went upstairs then and Allegradonna played with his new name as only a wife can.

As the dawn came slipping through the window, Andrea was still awake. He realized that he had allowed some space to come between himself and Allegradonna.

"I will do my best to always let you know what I am thinking, what I am doing, for you are my guiding star," he whispered to her sleeping form.

But she was not sleeping and she replied by kissing him, poking him lightly in the side, and leaping out of bed to start the day.

"Do not forget me, *Palladio*," she said, and rose to respond to Leonida, who had started squalling in his cradle.

Andrea realized this was the first time that anyone had ever called him by his new name, and smiled. It was fitting that his new name was spoken by his wife.

Trissino now began Palladio's education in earnest. Palladio studied the works of experts like Ceredi (hydraulics), Agricola (mineralogy), Tartaglia and Ramelli (applied mathematics), Belli (optical measurements), and Zarlino (geometrical musical harmony). He read poetry and learned about ancient Roman and Greek theater. Palladio was never seen without writing materials, a book, or a musical instrument.

He became a constant dinner companion at Trissino's house. Trissino kept a good table and he invited other men of wealth who were versed in everything from the military theory of Hadrian to the current cost of silk. Palladio, with his warm social abilities, was ensured a seat at every meal. The Barbaro brothers were frequent visitors as were the Thiene brothers, Marcantonio and Adriano; members of the Valmarana family; and the two Chiericati brothers, Girolamo and Giovanni.

These families ruled the city of Vicenza and held civic decisions in the palms of their hands. Trissino always made sure that Palladio was seated strategically near them, knowing that with wit and charm, he would make himself indispensable as a dinner guest, and hopefully in the future as an architect, for Palladio had revealed to Trissino his deepest wish: to be the best architect that Italy had ever seen.

Chapter Ten

1540: THE HOUSE OF GODI

Palladio, as he was now known, had become the focal point of communication for several large-scale projects. His drawings were maturing into a clean yet evocative style, and his ability to communicate clearly with noblemen about restrictions both logistical and financial became legendary.

Girolamo and Giovanni entertained their guests with daily accounts of Palladio's ability to woo the sometimes cranky noblemen. They often told the story of Palladio's first meeting with Valesco, a wealthy if somewhat ridiculed man whose understanding of art, literature, and poetry could be kept in a thimble. Girolamo and Giovanni, with no shortage of mischief, had asked Palladio to talk to Valesco because they had heard that he was not happy with the textured treatment on his front facade walls. They called Palladio into their studio and told him about the problem. They would accompany him, but they tasked Palladio with being responsible for their client's happiness.

Palladio stared at both of them in turn, wondering what new torture they had devised. They managed to stay serious and silent until Palladio left the room, and only then did they break down in laughter until they nearly cried, for Valesco was a known problem.

Girolamo, Giovanni, and Palladio drove out to the site of the new Valesco domicile. The day was warm, with swallows swooping overhead. They found Valesco staring up at the new wall, his eyes squinting in the summer sun.

"Why can't this be uniform?" he whined.

The wall was a series of elaborately hand-pocked stone sections. Each section had been pocked by a different workman, so of course each one was slightly different from the next.

Girolamo and Giovanni turned away and stared at the sky, pretending to suddenly see something there of interest.

Palladio had prepared his response. "It is about nature. For isn't man only a part of nature?" he asked reasonably. "And as in nature, no stone is alike. For every leaf shines as an individual even though its kin falls from the same tree."

Valesco looked at him, one eyebrow sullenly arched. He was not mollified. He stood there with his hands on his hips, his numerous large rings digging into his waistline.

"If I had wanted nature, I wouldn't have hired men," he said, clearly not buying Palladio's line.

Palladio ran his hand over the wall and tried another tack. "My dear honorable Valesco, each section is designed to reveal the amazing number of workmen that have contributed to your domicile. Hundreds, in fact. This wall clearly exhibits this—it is as though each man had signed his own name."

Valesco was still for a moment, taking in this new information. Palladio had heard that one never knew where things stood with Valesco, for he was a man who took his time before answering, and sometimes, when his answer finally burbled to the top, it did not have anything to do with the original train of thought.

Valesco finally spoke. "I have a horse that needs a strong hand, so I will attend to it now." And with that, he turned and headed in the direction of his stables.

Palladio sighed with relief. He had been ready for more ways to mollify Valesco. He had armed himself with other examples around town, comments about the beauty of the texture itself, and the fact that Madame Bruni, a favorite courtesan, had remarked about the wall's intriguing visual qualities. Instead the man needed to see about a horse. Palladio realized he actually felt a bit deflated. He had been prepared for a many-pronged intellectual battle.

On this day, Palladio was filled with trepidation, for Girolamo and Giovanni had insisted that this was his time to fly. He was to go to the meeting with the Godi brothers alone. Like the wren who is pushed out of the nest by his parents, he would either figure out how to use his wings or come crashing to the ground.

The Godis were a powerful Vicenzan family with a long history. The father of three boys, Enrico was a lawyer and a landowner, rich in wealth, prestige, and honor. He had succeeded in gaining the title of cavalier, a title that lifted him from merely a wealthy landowner to a man who had contributed to society in ways over and beyond family obligations and interests.

One of his sons, Girolamo, had received the primary responsibility of supervising and rebuilding a large swath of land northwest of Venice. He had been eyeing a hilltop near the Astico River, an area near the village of Lugo Vicentino. This was a place that received cooling breezes in the summer and the warmth of a pale winter sun. It had a foundation left over from a previous building that had burned down, which would determine the position of the planned villa.

The first time Palladio met the Godi brothers, Girolamo was eating sugared grapes while his two brothers, Pietro and Marcantonio, were sitting at the same table, silver wine goblets in hand. The three brothers had become uncommonly collegial since their father had passed away, making decisions together as though they were friends instead of family, and this day was no different. The men joked with each other like school pals, clapping each other on the back and laughing until tears ran from their eyes.

Girolamo offered Palladio one of his green sugared grapes. Palladio popped one into his mouth and had to resist the impulse to spit it out. Sugary to the point of being cloying, it was a struggle to choke it down. Palladio swallowed it in one sodden gulp. He had never heard of such a thing, and after tasting it, he thought he knew why. Rumor had it that Girolamo's grand passion was food, yet contrary to all who knew him and saw how much he ate, he was as thin as a post.

They were at the Godi *casa della città*, the townhouse that the brothers shared in the center of Vicenza. The room had an exquisite fresco: Life-sized figures of women and men bathing against an azure background dominated the room. Palladio noted that the work exhibited the newest technique of indenting the surface of the wall at the eyes. This made the eyes of the bathers seem pensive. It felt as though their minds were far away from the baths that they should have been enjoying. Palladio realized he was lost in the contemplation of that idea and had been daydreaming when Girolamo asked him which way he thought the house should face.

Palladio knew that this was a test. He had neither been out to the proposed site nor had the opportunity to study it. He demurred, carefully insisting that he needed to work in collaboration with Giovanni da Porlezza and Girolamo Pittoni. In truth, he was already the best draftsman in the shop and both Giovanni and Girolamo had grown to rely on his quick wit, able drawing skills, and pure likability.

Palladio wished that they had accompanied him. They would have leaned on their long history of working with the patrons of Vicenza. They would have listened and then managed to figure out a way to manipulate the conversation so they could squeeze in their thoughts and make the patrons believe they had thought those same thoughts first.

In reality, although Palladio was not aware of it, they knew that he was already a master at this art, too. But on this day, Palladio was cowed by the fraternity in front of him. The camaraderie that they shared made him feel inexperienced and young. Although he was in his early thirties, he felt like a child in front of these three. They never disagreed, but rather seemed to support each other in all thoughts. It was as though they were one person.

As a large meal of beef and rigatoni was served and Girolamo enthusiastically speared slice after slice of beef, he explained his vision. "The villa needs to be many things all at once: a barn, a silo, a home, a meeting house. It will need to speak power, functionality, grace. And it should be big, solid, like me!"

He stood up. His two brothers stood up as well and Palladio envisioned a wall made of flesh.

"Yes!" exclaimed Pietro. "It should look as though a giant had laid a rectangular egg!"

"Yes," Marcantonio chimed in. "Yes, and it should fit in with our barn that father built only four short years ago."

At the mention of their father, the three brothers crossed themselves in unison.

As Girolamo stuffed rigatoni into his cheeks, Palladio realized that he would not have much opportunity to have input into this house—his first real opportunity to show what he could do. As far as the three brothers were concerned, this was a house that would reflect their desires and designs. They were a united front of family, flesh, and familiarity and would have very little time to listen to a novice architect.

As he left the Godi house after this first initial meeting, he realized that he had never tasted the meal. The cloying after-taste of the sugared grape remained in his mouth. One thing was clear: This project would reflect the patrons more than the architect.

At first, this thought was a mournful one. Palladio sighed and thought about posterity. Would this building, a structure that represented the taste and ideas of three patrons rather than his own, go down in history as a failure? He shook his head as though willing the thought to fly out of his head and disappear. But more thoughts poured in, and with them, doubt.

He shared his doubts with Allegradonna. Sinking into the chair in front of the fire, he opened up. He felt old. He was over thirty. He was a man with a family, with responsibilities, yet here he was, being told what to do by three men who collectively knew less than he did. Would he always be the man on the lowest rung of the ladder? Always the man sent to calm the difficult patrons?

This building could destroy his career before it started. In Palladio's eyes it would lack continuity and form. It would be heavier than he would like and it would lack the new ideas that he was itching to put into practice.

Allegradonna let him talk and talk and talk, and said nothing. Then she built him back up brick by brick. She countered each one of his doubts by giving him a litany of his talents. It was as though she was applying mortar, strengthening his resolve, his faith.

Palladio felt renewed. After they spoke, he went out for a walk. He would take what he could learn from this project. He would build on the experience as surely as stones laid upon each other became a building. This idea cheered him. This project would be the first stone. His step lightened, and as he walked, he grabbed a leaf of mint that trailed from a flowerpot and popped it into his mouth. Within minutes, the sour taste was gone.

The Godi villa project was on schedule. The three brothers were on site inspecting the progress of the new family estate and were taking bets on when the villa would be completed. Giovanni thought that the family could move in the next spring, before Venice putrefied with heat, while Girolamo thought that it would be more than a year. They went around the back of the house to inspect the rest of the construction site, leaving Palladio to talk to Gianni, one of the workers, after he had descended from the scaffolding that surrounded the two stories. Gianni was a man who had been working with Girolamo, Giovanni, and Palladio for more than two years. He hailed from the Dolomites and was a talent with the rough white rock that was mined from those hills.

Gianni wiped his brow with a red cloth and drank from the ladle that Palladio offered him. He was as dark as the stone was white. He was thin and made up of sharp angles, but his manner was round and buttery and easygoing. He had caught the interchange on the soft wind that now ruffled his black curls and he smiled.

"Patrons come in as many colors as the stone with which we build their houses."

Palladio agreed, and they went on to discuss the installation of the brickwork that would surround the Ionic column next to them.

After they had finished their talk of business, Palladio asked Gianni, "What do you think? In terms of completion, do you side with Girolamo or with Giovanni?"

Gianni scratched the tip of his nose and said, "Giovanni. Absolutely. Giovanni." His red bandana was half falling out of his pocket.

Palladio tucked it back in and replied with a knowing smile. "Me too."

One summer evening, when the nightjars were in full throat, the topic at Trissino's table was the alphabet. The ten men dining came from a wide variety of backgrounds, but they all enjoyed talking about language. In 1524, Trissino had written an essay that scrutinized the letter "i" and created a new letter from it— the letter "j." Prior to this essay, there had been many exciting dinners where some of the men had almost come to blows over the extra "swash" at the bottom of the "i." Trissino had suggested that the swashed "i" be transformed into another letter and be called a "j." There was a need, for there were now many words that required a specific soft sound, a sound made when the tongue was briefly close to the roof of the mouth. With all of the Eastern trade that was transforming the purses of many of the men sitting at that very table, there was a need to be able to write down where some of these items came from. A good example was an area rich in silks and spices, an area called Beijing.

One of the men who sat on Trissino's right was a guest. He was a merchant from Venice, a silk trader who had picked up some of the languages in foreign ports. He raised a toast to Trissino, for without the letter "j," he would have been unable to write down many of the cities and provinces that spelled out where his silk trade came from.

Trissino happily took the compliment as the men at the table raised their glasses in his honor. Palladio was amazed. There were so many facets of Trissino that he was unaware of. Trissino and the men around him made the act of learning a serious business. There was nothing out of bounds and their thirst for knowledge was as normal to them as drinking water. Debate was seen as a healthy pursuit, and arguments occasionally got so heated that noses were bloodied. Palladio drank in the atmosphere like wine. He was where he wanted to be and he was with the people he wanted to be with.

The conversation turned to politics and military strategy, and some of the men began railing against Charles V, who had just returned to Rome from Algiers with his tail between his legs.

"He attempted it too late in the season," one man in a bright red doublet said with a belch. "He misjudged the weather and got caught out. No kind of sailor there."

"I blame Andrea Doria," said another. "The *condottiero* are only in it for one thing: money."

Palladio was amazed that these men talked so fearlessly about people in power.

"Charles V," spit out one man who looked like he was feeling a little bilious. "Too much responsibility for one man. The 'empire on which the sun never sets,' my eye. If he didn't have so much land to oversee, he could find out what is really going on."

"That's how people lose ships," added another, and the conversation moved on.

Palladio thought about this freewheeling discussion; how some people could freely talk about whatever they wanted to and how some could not.

That night he discussed this with Allegradonna. She surprised him when she looked him squarely in the eye and said, "Well, at least you are a man. As a woman, I am consigned to the role of supporter and mother."

Palladio sat back in his chair, stunned. He was amazed that he had never given this idea any thought before. There were never any women at their tables except those who served them, and they were certainly not sitting down and contributing to the conversation.

He gazed at Allegradonna in the firelight, and to his surprise he saw a tear course down her cheek. He reached up and wiped it tenderly away.

Chapter Eleven

1541: THE FIRST TRIP TO ROME

Palladio rode up to Trissino's stables. Two mules stood in the courtyard; a litter was suspended between them and in it sat Trissino, a bunch of green grapes in his hand. Two carts pulled by Ardennais draft horses carried tools, papers, and clothing. Trissino was as excited as a child and, when he saw Palladio, beckoned eagerly to him.

"Palladio! You are here at last! Come meet Marchello and Eduardo!" Trissino turned to address two men who stood nearby. "My cook and my priest, meet my new protégé, Palladio. Palladio! We will all go to Rome and explore. You, Marchello, my fine friend, will find yourself a new supply of excellent cheeses, and you, Eduardo, will be in charge of my soul. See that it does not slip any further!" He clambered down and properly introduced Palladio to two men whom he would grow to love.

Marchello, with his wild hair and salt-and-pepper beard, telegraphed his loose way with basil. He could coax an event out of a single goose. During their first dinner together, Palladio was amazed when Marchello, after an excellent meal of veal and onions, launched into a galliard, a lively dance with its five steps known as *cinque passi*. He turned and jumped high into the air and finally ended his manic dance with a cadence, a long leap which ended by going down on one knee in front of Trissino. Trissino loved this and flipped a gold coin high into the air, which Marchello caught in his cap.

Eduardo, Trissino's priest, was the understanding sort, capable of forgiveness, kindness, and legendary wine making. He had escaped a poor childhood by signing up for the priesthood at an early age. He was stout and devout and understood the frailties of humanity, therefore forgiveness was his overarching life theory. Before traversing any river, he and Trissino would unload a small altar. Eduardo scavenged for flowers while Trissino fetched the holy water from its special cabinet. Together, they knelt and prayed to St. Christopher, the patron saint of travelers, who had carried Christ himself over a river.

Palladio had never been to Rome before. His friends and family were almost as thrilled as he was. When Giovanni and Girolamo had heard of Trissino's offer, they had supported the trip on all levels. They knew it was like sending Palladio to school for four years. He would come back a much more skilled worker and designer, and they were excited to see how it would impact him.

All four men—Giovanni, Girolamo, Trissino, and Palladio—met and talked about what Palladio could learn, what he could bring back to the design studio. Palladio had an idea that he presented at this meeting. He wanted to measure, as much as humanly possible, the most beautiful ruins in the city. He had the idea that in measuring what remained of these buildings, he could uncover what made them so iconic. It would inform all of them.

Giovanni and Girolamo were aware of how much time he would need to take off, but they also recognized Palladio for what he could become: someone who had the potential to become a true artist. They would not stand in his way. And of course if he became a famous architect, they knew where he would go for his materials and labor.

Allegradonna, knowing that this might be a life-changing experience for him, handed him a large wheel of cheese as a going-away gift while little Leonida danced around his shins, sensing the excitement of the adults. His wife walked him to the door, with Leonida in her arms. As he turned to leave, Palladio saw an expression of love, but also envy, clear on her face.

Palladio had heard many stories about the beauty of Rome—its architecture, the vibrancy of the people, the deep color of the sky, and its seven hills. He thought he would be awestruck by the "Eternal City," as the Latin poet Tibullus called it, but he was wrong. It turned out to be even more than he could have dreamed of, for it was filled with jewels; buildings that seemed to speak only to him.

The four men—Trissino, Marchello, Eduardo, and Palladio—had begun their journey early after a quick breakfast of bread and cheese. With his usual natural aplomb, Marchello had readied the horses and organized the kitchen and the bedclothes in under an hour.

When at last they had reached the hill above Rome, Palladio let out a whistle of appreciation. The city was spread out before him, a visual gift that immediately filled his head with imagined smells and sounds. He could hear faint cries from vendors and drivers cursing and cajoling their oxen. Trissino pointed out the Basilica di San Clemente al Laterano, the Pantheon, the Santa Maria Sopra Minerva, and the Basilica di Santa Maria Maggiore. The Aurelian Walls snaked grandly around the city.

"The Aurelian Walls have 383 towers, 7,020 crenellations, eighteen main gates, five postern gates, 2066 external windows, and 116 toilettes," said Trissino grandly, exhibiting his excellent memory. "Brick-faced concrete. Sixteen meters high."

As they wove down the hill, they joined hundreds of other travelers making their way toward one of the gates of the city. Palladio was riding in one of the carts, sitting up with his back against a barrel, prepared with some drawing paper he had brought from home. As they neared the wall, he quickly started sketching. When his first drawing of Rome appeared under his hand, he started to feel guilty for using so much of the paper. Trissino's litter drew alongside him, and he mentioned this to Trissino. Trissino smiled, opening a drawer cleverly concealed in the litter that Palladio had not seen before. It was filled with paper.

"All yours," said Trissino, and went back to munching on a fig.

As their small procession flowed through the narrow archway, Palladio felt like a freshwater trout flowing through a sluice. When they had at last made it through to the other side, he was now a part of the city of Rome, the place he had longed to go to since he was a child.

They found themselves in a market—a very loud market. Children screamed, cried, and laughed; mothers and fathers scolded. Vendors were struggling with stumbling oxen, frightened horses, bleating sheep, flapping geese. Only the fish were silent in their glistening arrays.

Men from the Orient were plying spices in a language that Palladio had never heard before and the spices that wafted through the air made him sneeze. Moors were selling myrrh and frankincense, and the streets stank of manure. With difficulty, the group made their way through the crowds, aiming for the palace of Trissino's friend, the Venetian cardinal Marino Grimani.

During this trip, Palladio not only traveled to Rome, but also journeyed up through the ranks of class. Flying under the wings of Trissino, he was now a person that the wealthy were interested in talking to. He had access to some of the finest minds working in Rome at that time. Writers, painters, sculptors, archbishops, cardinals, generals, noblemen—Trissino seemed to have them all charmed and reeled in like the proverbial bream. The conversations at the dinner tables and in the sleepy arbors in the back gardens were filled with ideas that flowed into Palladio's waiting mind.

When Trissino took him to the three-storied Palazzo Farnese,

Palladio thought of a regiment of armies, neatly lined up like the windows in this astounding building. But it wasn't until he attended a late-night dinner that the depths of the design and the characters who had played a part in that design became clear.

At the end of the table, a large man with a barrel chest was worrying about the size of the crenellations. He was Antonio da Sangallo, the original architect of the building, and he was engaged in a serious debate with a man who sat across from the table, gesturing with a hunk of bread. The man with the bread was introduced to Palladio as Michelangelo di Lodovico Buonarroti Simoni, a sculptor, painter, architect, and poet who had been collaborating on the building for several years. He was rough and unkempt and constantly talked about leaving the dinner table because he needed to sleep, and yet he talked on.

Michelangelo, for that was how he was known, was defending his deep crenellations, citing that they gave visual interest to the building and that the shadows they created had been the missing natural element. "What is shadow without light? What is light without shadow?" he bellowed.

As Palladio listened, he marveled at Michelangelo's furrowed brow. Here was a man who made his living thinking deeply and acting on those thoughts—it was clearly written within those lines. Then Palladio laughed inwardly as he imagined a tiny farmer behind his ox, plowing the lines into Michelangelo's forehead.

Michelangelo moved on, now pushing the idea that a bridge needed to be built in the rear of the building so that it could be connected to the Vigna Farnese, land belonging to the Farnese family that was nestled across the Tiber River. The discussion about bridges and gardens and coats of arms went on until dawn broke, and it wasn't until Palladio felt Trissino's hand gently nudging him in the shoulder that he realized he had fallen sound asleep at the table. He had not completely lost face, however. The rest of the party had broken up long ago and only a few men were still at the table, now drinking strong coffee and standing up to leave as well.

That next morning, Palladio was eager to begin his real work: that of measuring and resurrecting some of the grand buildings of Rome. He had brought his circumferentor, a kind of surveyor's compass. Nine months after Trissino had taken him in as a protégé, Trissino had given it to him as a gift. It was one of Palladio's prized possessions. It was housed in a brass box and contained a magnetic needle that spun and wheeled around eight sectors, always seeking north. When he put it on the legs that he had carved for it, he could measure horizontal angles with ease.

Trissino took him past the Forum to an area that was a series of broken stone walls. When Trissino told him it was the ruins of the Baths of Agrippa, within Palladio's mind walls began to grow from the rubble.

Palladio knew that the art in architecture was in seeing the swallow before it flew, the oak before it grew, the building before a single stone was laid. To imagine something that was not there was either the vision of a madman or an artist. In the former, it was a burden, a disaster. In the latter, it was a gift.

Palladio put the gift to good use when viewing these ruins.

It was a combination of the analytical and the sublime, the engineered and the imagined. His technique was simple. First, he would measure, observe, and notate. How big was this corner stone? What were its proportions? What was it made of? He wrote everything down.

And then he imagined that the wall continued, that the door opened and beckoned him through to the inside. When Palladio saw the ways that the floors were laid out, the gridded pattern of the old stones lying in regular squares, he could also see the Romans. When they were at their best, for example in the public baths, there was democracy, for generals bathed with butchers, noblemen soaked with silversmiths. They breathed the same steam, cupped the same water, and cleared the dirt of the day off of their faces together. And when they could not stand the steamy heat any longer, they strolled through the same gardens and viewed the same statues posing within the curved arbors.

He assembled his circumferentor and began the work of surveying the ruins that were all that remained of these splendid baths.

Palladio knew about them, of course. Everyone held them up as a premium example of humanist architecture, as the baths were available to all. The Romans had used a clever series of aqueducts, the Acqua Vergine, that channeled water throughout the city and diverted it for an extensive series of inviting pools.

The baths, also known as the laconium, had been filled with a variety of places to soak. There was the frigidarium (the cold pool), the tepidarium (the lukewarm pool), and the caldarium (the hot pool). In addition to these areas of supreme soaking, there were also areas to sit in the sun, colonnades to walk through, life-sized statues to marvel at—everything that could make a person feel as though they were part of a city, part of a culture, part of something larger than themselves.

This is what Palladio himself aspired to. He was, after all, a man of the people. If his life had taken a different turn, he would be in Padua at that moment, grinding grain at his father's mill. He had been lucky, for he had found a route to the arts and an opportunity to create large-scale buildings for the enjoyment of all. *What better way to spend one's life*, he thought as he rolled up his sleeves and began to set up his instruments.

He would measure the ruins carefully, learn as much as possible, and then use the firmaments to create new designs. This method would allow him to include the mathematical precision and proportions of the Romans as well as the ideas that were percolating in his head.

At that moment, a methodology began forming that would transform not only the area of Vicenza and Venice, but the world.

When Palladio saw the Pantheon, he fell in love. Eight columns welcomed him in, and when he stepped into the colossal portico, he involuntarily gasped. Two layers of archways and windows started from the ground, but it was the patterned dome yawning over him that impressed. Trissino remarked that it was as high as it was tall, forty-three meters, and that it was rumored to be unreinforced. The oculus, the open hole at the top of the simple dome, allowed light and life to pour into the building.

At that moment, it began to rain and water poured through the open hole. It was like being under a waterfall. People scattered and shrieked. Palladio did just the opposite. He ran toward the torrent that splashed on the marble floor and dove in. He found himself with his face aimed at the oculus, standing in the rain, getting drenched. He raised his arms toward the sky and imagined that God was watching him. Trissino looked on, enjoying the view of this young man, his arms lifted to the heavens.

As part of Palladio's education in Rome, Trissino made sure to take his protégé to as many plays as possible, as Trissino had a special place in his heart for theater. They saw *Oedipus Rex, Lysistrata,* and a new play that used real horses. Because all of the ancient theaters of Rome were long gone, these productions were performed in temporary wooden structures that were built for limited runs. Palladio liked these excursions; Trissino inevitably became an enchanted child of ten, insisting that they sit in the front row so they would get the full impact. When the horses were onstage, they were hit with sweat from both the horses and the actors.

Palladio and Trissino also visited the Temple of Hadrian, the Basilica of Maxentius, the Temple of Clitumnus, the Temple of Vesta at Tivoli, and the Dioscuri in Naples. At every place they stopped, they pitched tents and prepared for a week's stay.

Marchello was an expert marksman and would furnish them with rabbit and stag, and the markets were filled with a delectable assortment of breads, fruits, and meats. After a full day of lying down on the ground, climbing up columns, and scrambling around fallen pedestals, Palladio would have a difficult time staying awake. But Trissino's tables always groaned under a cornucopia of food as well as ideas, and it was painful to think that he might miss anything, so he often pushed himself toward the table.

The trip to Rome changed Palladio forever. He had traveled to mecca and had seen the building of his dreams: the Pantheon. He had touched its rough stones, stood in its yawning space, and bathed in an afternoon shower where he was both inside and outside at the same time. He had stood where Vitruvius had stood and breathed in the same air. The ruins had charmed him with their mystery and elegance. History and the present blended seamlessly. He had been introduced to thinkers, artists, writers, and priests. Philosophy and wit were blended with wine and veal, the chemistry of paint had been endlessly discussed, and he had seen grown men cry after hearing an epic poem.

All of his experiences had solidified a new way of thinking. A new way of approaching his craft. He would take what he saw and what he imagined, and, using the elements of classic architecture, he would create something new. With his hands, mind, and eyes, what was once old would live again.

Months passed before Palladio and Trissino made their way back to Vicenza. Allegradonna greeted her husband at the front door with an expression of welcome, but as he kissed her, Palladio thought he saw something else in her eyes. He knew that his absence was hard on her and he gave her another kiss, this one more tender than the first. Initially, Leonida hardly recognized his father and he stood shyly behind his mother's skirts until Palladio gave him a small gift: a new orange ball. Allegradonna treated him to a special chicken *cacciatore* dinner, and it was not until they were alone in bed together did she reveal her surprise: She was pregnant.

Trissino made dining his own art form. He had adopted many of the new trends that were making the act of eating such a pleasant experience. He had silver plates instead of the usual wooden ones or, worse yet, bread, which in most poorer households was used in lieu of a plate. He favored the fork, a new utensil designed expressly to get the food from the table to the mouth with as little fuss as possible. He had a credenza, a special piece of furniture designed to hold the food before the servants served it, and he often featured a musical *intermezzo* that would allow the gentlemen to stretch their legs between courses.

One autumnal night, a visitor introduced a new substance that was filtering into Venice. He called it tobacco and it was being touted as a new healthy way to stay warm. That night they all tried it during the intermezzo, but the coughing and retching had proven it a distinct failure.

On an afternoon not long after the night of tobacco, Trissino teased Palladio with a note about a surprise special guest who would be attending his dinner that night. Palladio and Allegradonna speculated as to who it could be. In truth, Palladio scarcely cared, for the dinner table at Trissino's was always an exercise in splendor, both in terms of the experience as well as the company. Allegradonna, although she missed Palladio when he went off to these dinners, always welcomed the food that he brought back home.

As Palladio knocked on Trissino's door, he heard the laughter of his friends coming from the open window on the main floor, the piano nobile. Some healthy argument was propelling the voices to loud volumes. As the servants let him in, he hastened up the stairs, not wanting to miss anything.

He entered a room filled with the laughter, banter, and arguments. Long strings were being strung out horizontally through the air. The end of each strand was attached to an edge of a chair on the far side of the room. The other ends were being bundled up in a handful and each man was taking a turn looking along the strands as though looking through a spyglass. The room was animated with men jostling each other to get the opportunity to look down the strings and toward the chair. One servant's assignment was to move the chair slightly when asked to. Each time he did, the man with the bundled string laughed. As Palladio listened, he realized that the word "perspective" was carpeting the room, for almost every man in the room was talking about it.

He knew most of the men, but at the far end of the table, the place reserved for special guests, was a man he had never seen before. He was slight of frame with puffs of thin hair that curled in gentle curves on his forehead. A well-trimmed goatee and a healthy if somewhat unruly moustache made his babyish face look even more smooth. There was not one line, not one angle to the man, and his cheekbones were covered with soft pads of flesh. Palladio was taken with his eyes, for they were kind and soft. The four-layer ruff that framed his face made him look even less grown up, almost like a boy dressed in man's clothing.

He was excitedly gesturing, calling out suggestions. It was clear it was he who had introduced this new parlor game.

Trissino introduced him as Sebastiano Serlio, an architect from Venice who was on his way to France to create a building for the king, Francis the First. Palladio bowed. He remembered that day so long ago when Giovanni had shown him Serlio's theatrical drawings. Here was a man he greatly admired, in the flesh. Serlio had written *On Architecture*, the five-book illustrated treatise that was filled with subjects that were dear to Palladio's heart: geometry, perspective, and detailed descriptions of old Rome—baths, palazzos, temples, arches.

When he had seen the book in Rome, it had only been published a few years and there were not many copies available for purchase. Palladio had immediately sat down in the bookmaker's shop and dived in. Many hours later, Trissino had only been able to get Palladio to leave the shop by buying the book for him. It was one of Palladio's prized possessions and here was the man who had authored it, standing before him.

The men soon tired of the perspective game and retired to the table to begin eating in earnest. Palladio had the pleasure of being seated at Serlio's left hand, so he was able to talk with him at length. Serlio was childlike in his behavior as well as his appearance, with a piping high voice. This day he was especially happy for he had been invited to help design a new area that would be attached to the Château de Fontainebleau, already a monumental palace.

The king wished to build a new group of buildings that would define a large courtyard. He wanted an expansive park, new pavilions, and a grotto. He had already brought Rosso Fiorentino to create frescoes for a new gallery, and he was eager to have Serlio design a wing that would bring together the northern wing of the Ministers, the new southern wing of the gallery dedicated to Ulysses, and the eastern wing of Ferrare. If Serlio could do all of this, his reputation would be certain.

Palladio reassured him. He placed his hand on Serlio's blue velveted arm. "The five books have already assured you a place in history."

In the midst of the chaos born of twelve half-drunk and intelligent men, this comment stilled Serlio. He began musing about the concept of immortality, saying that it was what drove most artists. It was a kind of heaven on earth, he said, for one's name would be spoken through the centuries, and if one were lucky, one would be remembered, perhaps forever, for the monuments they had designed, the paintings they had created, the books they had written.

Years later, when Palladio remembered that day, he often thought about the truth of that still moment. The softness in Serlio's eyes had reflected the candlelight and Palladio thought he'd seen an escaped tear. Perhaps he had been clairvoyant, for Serlio never got the chance to design in France or anywhere else ever again. In four years, he was dead.

Chapter Twelve

1542: BEGINNING *THE FOUR BOOKS OF ARCHITECTURE*

Palladio was at his desk in front of his second-story window. He had taken tips from Trissino, who was a hearty proponent of the printing press and had decided to write a book. A book was a way to communicate, a way to share. A book could be carried to the four corners of the earth. Palladio knew that it would be an effort that would take him a lifetime, so he might as well start now. He would do it in between home and work, between dinners, after the candles in the house were otherwise extinguished. Hopefully it would ensure his legacy.

He had begun with the title page: *The Four Books of Andrea Palladio's Architecture, Wherein, After a Short Treatise of the Five Orders, Those Observations That Are Most Necessary in Building, Private Houses, Streets, Bridges, Piazzas, Xisti, and Temples Are Treated Of.* He thought the page should be ornate with trumpeting angels and maidens wielding the tools of the trade—a ruler, a square, calipers, and a protractor. It would include several glowering corbel heads and four detailed columns.

He wondered about the books. What would each one be? Perhaps the First Book would focus on materials: where to get them, how to process them, which ones to choose. This book would be so simple that it would make the average person want to create their own terrazzo floor. Or mix their own bricks. Or choose and lay their own stones for the fireplace.

The Second Book could be all about residencies, both the ones he would succeed in getting built as well as—

He stopped short. What could he call the buildings that existed only in his mind?

He looked out of the window. For weeks he had been watching as a pair of swallows built their mud-daubed nest under one of the eaves. They were winged brick layers, carefully building a pocket made of small mud pellets. In a way, he envied them. They would build their house and live in it, raise their chicks, and finally die, leaving their house to crumble away. He wondered if he would ever live in a house of his own design.

Then, unbidden, the word "invention" sprang to mind. It was likely that many of the drawings would exist only in his imagination; buildings he had designed but might never get the opportunity to see in real life. They would exist in the book and perhaps someday the drawings would be built, long after he was dead. It was like Serlio's idea—a way to beat death. He laughed uneasily, wondering if this was a concept that was godless or full of God. He shrugged the thought away and moved on.

The Third Book would cover public structures: roads, baths, bridges, basilicas, piazzas. Each book would seize the imagination and provide intricate elevations that would not only raise the building, but also uplift the mind.

Yet it would be the Fourth Book that would charm readers with imagination and spirituality. For in this book, Palladio would defeat the carnage of war, the wreckage of time, and the pain of neglect, and resurrect the temples of ancient Rome. All of that time spent scrambling around ruins, taking copious measurements, and noting every design detail of every small fallen stone would be put to use. This book would combine imagination with discipline, artistry with tenacity.

With the help of Vitruvius's earlier book, Palladio would resurrect huge areas of the city, focusing on the temples long since crumbled and lost. It would be a kind of miracle, for he would be able to bring something that was long dead back to life. Again, he suffered a small shuddering doubt: Was this blasphemous? He took a few moments to search the depths of his heart and mind. No. This was in service of both men and God. He pressed on.

He worked with an ebony nib. The nib was inkless and designed to be used to press a ghostly crease into the paper. This crease could be gone over later with black gall ink made from oak apples. He used a ruler to make sure that the initial lines were straight. He took satisfaction when his sleeve, moving across the handmade paper, created a very slight shushing sound. For him it was a kind of prayer, this *sh*. It said *Hush now, you are working; hush, for you are focused and nothing will make you lose your focus.*

This was a necessary discipline, for without it, one line could go wrong, disrupting and ruining the entire page. This kind of watermarked paper was expensive, so Palladio worked with care.

In some ways, he was happiest while working on his book. There were no other voices he had to listen to other than his own. He could sequester himself and while away the hours with his ruler, drawing the lines to create shadows that would make the stone look three dimensional. Along the edges of the pages he included the sepulchral cow skulls, bucrania, and cornucopias filled with grapes, melon, carrots, tomatoes, and corn. He drew geometric designs and florets and took pleasure in drawing the statues, which had a breezy quality about them as though they all stood in a light and embracing wind. He felt that his females had an especially winsome quality about them. Palladio had taken a kind of mischievous pride in those statues, for he drew them as though they were having a grand time adorning the rooftops of some of these buildings.

He put the pen down reluctantly when he heard Allegradonna's call that dinner was being served. Although he loved his drawings, he loved his family more, and he reminded himself of this as he went downstairs.

Chapter Thirteen

1545: VILLA PISANI

The Villa Pisani started as many projects started: with lunch. It was September 1542, and Vettor Pisani and his new bride sat at one end of the table, while a host of men that Palladio did not know crowded around the rest of the table, reaching for more wine and swallowing down prodigious amounts of bread and cheese. These men were from Venice, and Palladio thought that they brought with them a kind of cosmopolitan air. They made him remember his humble roots.

His friend and employer, Giovanni, introduced him to one man in particular, a man with a red beard, who stood with his head cocked at such a tilt that Palladio could actually see up his nose. This was a man who saw the world through the lens of birthright and his only talent was that of immediately sensing when someone had not enjoyed an upper-crust upbringing. He spurned Palladio by refusing to talk to him, even after Palladio had asked him a pleasant question about the weather.

When Giovanni saw this interchange, he took the man by the elbow, and with a hand strengthened by years of stone carving, steered the man to the other end—the lesser end—of the table. Palladio saw Giovanni use the effect of his height to tower over the man, who seemed to puff up. Moments later he deflated after Giovanni said something in his ear.

When Giovanni rejoined their end of the table, he clapped Palladio on the back. Palladio never knew what Giovanni had said to the man with his nose in the air.

Girolamo—Palladio's other employer and Giovanni's partner—had watched this interchange as though it were a bit of theater, and with the air of a studied librarian, he pretended that nothing untoward had happened. The incident was like one drop of rain in a downpour for the room was full of noise. Marco and Daniele Pisani, Vettor's brothers, were loud and boisterous, filled with plans for their new estate, and Daniele Barbaro, whom Palladio knew well, had just arrived in Vicenza.

Vettor's bride was a stocky dark-haired woman with a smile that lit up her face whenever she looked at her new husband. Similarly, Vettor paid slight attention to the conversation that was going on around him, mostly staring at his new wife with a mixture of awe and love. Palladio always enjoyed being around newlyweds. It was like basking in a soothing bath. Soon, however, much to his disappointment, they departed, the two of them leaving an audible trail of loving sentiments behind them.

The men at Palladio's table began talking about rice. Marco and Daniele Pisani, fresh from a long trip that included the Orient, excitedly described this new crop.

"Look at this," Marco said with a flourish, and held out a small vial filled with seeds that resembled maggots.

A portly man in a red velvet vest grabbed it out of his hand and held it to the window so he could see it in the light.

Marco took the vial back, determined to keep track of the object even after so many glasses of wine. "You should see this crop in the fields. It is like looking at a lake and the workers are knee deep in water when they tend it. It can be had in Venice, but it is expensive. Why not grow it here?"

Trissino joked, "Such a good crop to grow in Venice!"

Everyone roared for they could all envision the Grand Canal choked with rice plants. Daniele would not be deterred; he continued to describe this crop from the Orient that could, with enough water, grow in the Mediterranean climate.

Palladio started to translate this conversation into the design of the estate, which was emerging in his imagination. "The Guá River is not far and you might be able to reroute some of its waters for the rice fields," he mentioned offhandedly.

"Yes! Yes!" Marco replied enthusiastically. "This rice requires regular flooding. You are a genius, Palladio!"

Then Daniele Barbaro, who had been idly eating black olives, chimed in. "Have you heard of this new dish, *risotto alla Milanese*? It was invented by a creative cook to celebrate the construction of the Milan Cathedral." He rubbed his stomach in fond memory. "I ate this dish in an osteria in Venice. It was colored with saffron. The owner said that it had been added to the dish as a joke. A joke! He said it was a reflection of the cathedral's stained-glass windows which were rumored to also have also been stained with saffron. It was delicious! What do you think? Do you think that they would have stained the windows with saffron?"

"Yes! Undoubtedly!" Marco chirped. "What is more natural? Think donkey dung!"

The rest of the men huffed and laughed at the reference.

Palladio now laid out a question as though laying down a gauntlet. "Does the same dish taste better in a well-designed room?" And then before anyone could reply, he answered his own question. "Yes! There is no doubt in my mind."

Trissino said, "This is very hard to prove. Aren't we almost always in different rooms eating different foods? Is there anyone who can tell a tale of having eaten the same food in two vastly different rooms?"

Daniele said in his slow, thoughtful voice, "I once had cassata in two places: once in my mother's house, and then I carried it to the alley outside and ate the rest of it. I would swear that the candied pears tasted sour when in the alley outside."

"Let me ask you, Daniele, what was in the alley?" Trissino smiled a little and Palladio knew what was on his mind.

"Well, there was a barrel of rancid fish oil, I remember that very well, and a dog who had just finished up his business right in front of me."

The room collapsed into gales of laughter.

"Perhaps the smell of rancid fish and dog excrement might have something to do with it, dear brother? Unless mother smells just as bad?" Marco managed to ask the question before disintegrating into high-pitched screams.

Giovanni actually fell to the floor and disappeared under the table. Palladio could hear him gasping between his laughs, which were as sonorous as snores.

Trissino, normally a sober individual, could not stop himself from crying. It was as though he had taken his thumb from the dike, for laughter streamed down his cheeks. He ended up with his head on the table as though all of the fluids that had poured from him had sapped him of any energy.

Such a level of hilarity cannot be sustained for any length of time, however, and they finally calmed down enough to return to the business at hand.

Daniele was the first to regain his composure. He took a few calming breaths, wiped his face with his cloak, and described the site. "Enough. I will die if we laugh any more. Let me tell you about our land." His eyes gleamed as he painted his picture. "In addition to our rice fields, our estate will have beautiful apple and peach orchards, flowing vineyards, and flowered terraced gardens that will be perfect for evening strolls. Don't you think, Marco?" He turned to his brother, who was still slightly puce. "We want to be able to train a horse and seduce a lovely lady in the same day, don't you think?"

Marco nodded, this time with less enthusiasm, but then added, "I will train so many horses!" He grabbed a chicken wing. "We had a main building, you know, originally, but it burned down, I think from a single candle that was left too close to a tapestry. Can I please have some drawing materials?"

A servant rushed away and brought him a quill, inkwell, and paper. Marco drew a picture of the many agricultural buildings that were left, including a blocky main building, two dovecotes, stables, and a *barchessa*, or barn. Palladio watched over his shoulder and admired Marco's sure style of drawing. *He must have had some training*, he thought, for the resulting quick sketches were full of verve and emotion.

Daniele added, "And we have a foundation for you to build on, which will be quite an advantage, don't you think?"

Palladio knew he was thinking of costs and nodded in agreement.

The Pisanis liked Palladio, and Giovanni had produced a splendid coat of arms for their father, so the conversation soon became one of money. Both Giovanni and Giacomo were skilled businessmen and Palladio always studied them, drinking in the way they flowed in and through the most difficult part of any project.

Palladio stared at the fine drawing. He could see the trees, the way that they would frame the building, the rusty terracotta roof, the long row of arches. He could hear the shout of the apple harvesters in the fruit trees calling for new bags, the kitchen maids as they called for eggs, the chickens themselves as they scratched for worms in the dirt. He had changed considerably since he had returned from Rome. He had a new confidence and was firmly convinced that his ideas were good. Although outwardly he remained calm and cool, he was a man on fire.

Visions of his recent visit to Rome organized the disparate buildings in front of him. He would link them all together so that instead of being a collection of odd buildings without any relationship to each other, they would become a unified whole.

The effect would be appropriately grand. He would raise the main building up so that the maids, footmen, stewards, valets, butlers, grooms, gardeners, and gamekeepers would have a place to get out of the rain and get warm and the cooks and maids would have a place to ply their craft. Raising the first floor would add to the overall impact: People would know that the building housed an important and wealthy family.

Chapter Fourteen

1543: RIDOLFI'S WELCOME

In September, Vicenza welcomed Cardinal Niccolò Ridolfi, who was arriving to take control of the local dioceses. Trissino, Daniele Barbaro, and Palladio were determined to let the cardinal know that they respected the wonders of God by creating a route that was filled with statues, arches, and painted panels filled with religious and welcoming inscriptions. These men made up a happy threesome for they had similar tastes, enjoyed each other's approach to life, and were able to accomplish more as a team than as individuals.

The process had been elaborate. Daniele had managed and partially financed the effort, while Palladio had been kept busy churning out plan after plan of statues and arches that would be made of wood and stucco—architecture that would only have to look good from the front and could reveal its theatrical roots in the back. For his part, Trissino kept the coffers full with an expansive table of dinner guests and a narrative that described the project in colorful, powerful terms.

The procession started with the cardinal and a cavalcade of dignitaries rolling under an enormous wood and stucco arch festooned with garlands, rosettes, and Ionic pillars. They turned into a courtyard filled with sound; water poured from amphorae that were held by two statues representing the Retrone and Bacchiglione Rivers. As they proceeded along their way, two giant statues, Happiness and Security, welcomed them before they drove under a double fronted arch and emerged in the main square to see a large rotating machine, The Wheel, ridden by yet another statue, Fortune.

The cardinal waved as people cheered alongside the street, flinging roses and jasmine into his coach. As he passed by, Palladio noted that his face was gentle and seemed to be used to smiling, as the area from his nose to his mouth was deeply lined.

This was a man whom Trissino, Daniele, and Palladio wanted to court, for not only was he a man of power, but also a man of vision. Unlike some cardinals whose only interests were in fine tables and comfort, Cardinal Ridolfi was a man who appreciated the arts and letters. He had a fine collection of artworks and a large library that housed many contemporary works as well as ancient texts. He was an excellent dinner guest for he could speak authoritatively on topics as obscure as the Asian art of calligraphy to the sewing techniques used on his own vestments.

Trissino knew him well. He and Palladio had visited him in his villa at Bagnaia where they had discussed the issue of aqueducts: How does one design an aqueduct that carries water *up* a hill? That was the question of that day and they pondered it in one of the cardinal's famous gardens. Ridolfi had explained that they had done this by building a tall hill. When the water came down from the higher hill it would create a kind of siphon, propelling the water up the second hill with the use of gravity and water pressure.

Their voices had ebbed and flowed with the numerous water fountains that dotted the formal gardens. The cardinal was a devotee of water fountains and pools. The pools had a special shadowy character—they were made of a volcanic stone called peperino, which, when wet, was the color of black pepper.

They had gone on to discuss the techniques of raising silk-worms and the trouble with raising sheep and what stars were made of. The cardinal was the godfather to Trissino's own brother and one of his sons, and he asked about them. Trissino ducked the question and instead diverted the conversation, asking why streams flowed down but rarely up. Palladio looked at his friend and wondered how such a man could have such a son.

The Pisani building was coming along. Palladio entered through the front facade, briefly examining the rusticated outer wall on his way in. He passed through the *loggia*, the long covered room open to the air, and entered the *sala*, the main room with a high vaulted ceiling. Workmen were adding stucco to the walls with flat paddles. A shivery winter light came through the thermal window, a half circle divided into three openings, and the work-men were armed against the chill with lengths of cloth wound around their heads.

He was pleased with the way the arching barrel-vaulted ceilings looked, so reminiscent of some of the vaults he had seen in Rome. Tilers on scaffolds, which raised them high up near the ceiling, were at work installing a delicate filigree design in orange, green, and red. When completed, each surface on the arch would include some sort of decoration. The thermal window shape was repeated by the curve of the vault, which pleased him no end.

Palladio smiled. This was his first real design. It had stepped from the flat dimension of the page to a building that would eventually be lived in, loved in, and died in.

When the room was complete, he wanted to bring the brothers and the new bride into the space and complete the bet they had made nearly two years before. Would food taste better in this lovely room? He knew it would.

Chapter Fifteen

1545: A VISIT TO VENICE

Palladio's relationship to Giovanni and Girolamo's design studio had gradually changed, and in truth, Palladio now functioned mostly as a free agent. He had been under the tutelage of Trissino for years now and enjoyed an existence free of formal bosses and instead filled with colleagues and patrons.

For Palladio's thirty-seventh birthday, Trissino proposed a trip to Venice. He knew that Venice represented an important part of Palladio's education and would open up new opportunities, for Venice was a city of enormous wealth. Everyone agreed that it was truly a shame that Palladio had not made the trip before.

Allegradonna was a little less enthusiastic. By now, they had five children and she often found herself overwhelmed by them. She was stirring a pot of *panada*, an inexpensive bread soup, when Palladio gave her the news.

She turned and waved a spoon at him threateningly. "Once again, you leave me, Andrea! Once again!"

Palladio untied her apron, took her by the hand, and led her to the chair before the fire.

"Venice means work for me. I will design one of those palaces along the Grand Canal and we will be able to afford a house of our own. We will eat like royalty and you will have so many dresses, you will need a special room to keep them in."

She looked at him and her brown eyes showed that she was not fooled. Money was always in short supply and she did not see a future that would be any different. But when he kissed her, she kissed him back, for this is what a wife did. And she knew that unlike many of her less fortunate friends, she was married to a good man.

Venice was like no other city. It was a combination of water, stone, and sky that was animated with gulls, horses, boats, dogs, chickens, and so many people that Palladio had trouble knowing where to step next. People were a tapestry that lay upon the landscape. They were shouting and pushing, crying and laughing, and there was even one small boy peeing in the corner. They were selling earthen pots from Istanbul, prosciutto on long sticks, jewelry that sparkled in the sun, and treasures from the Aegean—cuttlefish, eel, cod, and crab, some so fresh that they were still moving.

Baskets of produce had been carried in by mules until

the streets became too narrow even for them. Then men had taken them up, carrying them upon their shoulders to flat-bottom boats that were favored for the transportation of goods. These boats were brilliant with color, laden with dark green zucchini; bulbous avocados; green, yellow, and red peppers; garlic as big as a man's fist; white and purple onions; and bunches of orange carrots with scraggly bright green tops.

The air was filled with a universe of exotic smells—sandalwood, myrrh, frankincense, and curries. Palladio was startled to see a woman of the Orient—the first he had ever seen—with a long black braid down the back of her gold silk robe. Trissino laughed and remarked that Palladio looked like a fish with his mouth agape. Palladio quickly closed his mouth, but still found himself rapidly pivoting his head around so as to see all of these unusual sights.

People came from everywhere as this was a merchant city. They came in all colors, all body types; they resembled the variety of fruits and vegetables that lay on the slanted tables before them. And all the languages! Everyone seemed to be talking at each other, making themselves understood with active pantomime and exhibiting gestures of pure frustration. The only lingua franca was numbers, for the merchants carried boards with them that they could use to name prices and payments. Palladio thought about the Tower of Babel, imagining it as a curving series of stones that reached toward the heavens. What must the construction have been like to sustain such a height?

Upon entering the city, Trissino had stabled all of the horses and carts. Venice, with its labyrinthian streets, some only as wide as a man, was more easily accessed by the various ribbons of canals that allowed the transportation of goods and passengers. Everyone carried something, even Trissino, who held a treasured bottle of wine that was a gift for his host. Palladio carried his most precious tools for he would trust them to no one, not even the responsible Marchello.

Marchello flagged down a flat-bottom punt that would take most of their belongings and Trissino caught the eye of the gondolier who had been dispatched to pick them up. With the assistance of this short, slender man who looked more like a horseback rider than a boatman, Palladio and Trissino carefully stepped into the boat. The gondolier saluted Trissino and got them settled. Instead of opting for the *felze*, the inside cabin that had been adorned with purple tassels and red silk curtains, they chose to be outside in order to see the sights.

They took off down the Grand Canal, the major thoroughfare of Venice. The waterway was clogged with boats of all sorts, each designed for a specific task. The boats were steered by remarkable navigators, for despite being in close quarters, they rarely banged into each other. Instead, they streamed up and down the canal like capable mallards.

But it was the palaces lining the canal that intrigued Palladio. Each one seemed more fabulous than the next, with three- and four-storied facades that immediately faced the canal. The palazzos were built right where the canal edge began. A maid could empty a chamber pot out of the third-story window and it would land in the canal. However, this kind of behavior was punishable by a prison sentence, for many a nobleman had suffered a night ruined by an unfortunate downpour.

Palladio was later given a detailed lesson in the Venetian ways of sewage treatment. It was frowned upon to toss anything out of the windows and into the canal. Instead, the designers of Venice had created masonry tunnels that poured directly into the canals. The tides flowed in and out twice a day, freshening the canal as they did so. The theory, Palladio supposed, was that some things were better "sight unseen."

Trissino likened the palazzos to intricate jewels strung around the neck of the Grand Canal. The colors alone were stunning. Creamy eggshell whites, delicate peaches, filmy blues the color of the sky. And the details! Windows that claimed every nation—Syria, Abyssinia, Persia, Turkey, Moldova, China. The pointed lancet arch was joined by the intricate trefoil arch. The *extrados*, the curve formed by the outer edge of the windows, was sometimes Byzantine, reflecting the Orient, but some had a rounded Roman shape, particularly on the *intrados*, or inside edge.

Even the chimneys were unusual, with octagonal bell shapes placed on top of the flue. When Palladio remarked on their peculiar shapes, Trissino erupted into a lecture. Palladio thought, *What doesn't this man know about?*

"The flues on the inside of the house usually start in the piano nobile," explained Trissino, "where heat is needed during the cold of the winter months. It is supported by two brackets and arches, usually of Istrian stone and brick. The flue exists in a kind of netherworld, half in and half out of the wall."

Palladio thought about that for a moment. To exist half in and half out of the same world. Perhaps that was what it was like to be an angel. Or a demon.

"The mortar used is specially designed to withstand heat and the salt air. *Magra di marmorino.* This is a thin mixture that consists of one gallon of slaked lime, three gallons of white marble powder sieved to 0.7-millimeter granules, one quart of impalpable marble powder, and one quart of ground roof tiles." He ticked off these ingredients like he was remembering how to bake a cake.

Again, Palladio resolved to retain as much information in his head as his mentor did.

Then Trissino made some joke about and Titian and Giorgione, two competitive painters who had both attempted to create works on the bell shapes—and that it was a better thing to paint on the canvases of individual chimney bells than to war over paintings like *The Sleeping Venus.*

Trissino sat back, enjoying his pontification. "The bells themselves are of an ingenious design born out of a fear of fire. If a fire breaks out in Venice there is very little escape."

The gondolier looked at him and then quietly made the sign of the cross.

Trissino waved toward the buildings that lined the canal. "As you can see, most of the buildings are connected, so if one building catches on fire, it is likely that their neighbors will suffer as well." He paused a moment, then continued with a new thought. "The city used to be known for its intricate glasswork, but at the end of the thirteenth century, the glassworks were outlawed and forced to the island of Murano," he said, gesturing southeast.

Palladio made a mental note to visit this fabulous place and he envisioned that the island itself was made of shimmering glass.

"In normal chimneys, like those of Vicenza," Trissino said, laying a hand on Palladio's arm for emphasis, "the embers shoot straight out into the sky and can land anywhere, wreaking havoc like little hornets. In these bell-shaped chimneys, however, the sparks bounce around and around within the chamber itself and burn out harmlessly, unable to flee the confines of the bell."

As they continued down the canal, Palladio mused for a moment about the power of fire to destroy and create. Such a mercurial element, one that under the control of man is so useful, so necessary, yet one that when out of control is a torrent, a hideous destroyer of people and property. He resolved to look into these peculiar chimney tops further. He was interested in how architectural shapes manipulated not only people, but also air. And even the elements. He added fire to his growing list.

At last they docked in front of the magnificent four-story palazzo owned by the Barbaro family. Palladio counted twenty-nine windows, six balconies, and eighteen ocular depressions. It seemed to float on the water, a decorative gift box with a flat facade. Palladio marveled at the numerous windows, some with Gothic arches and some with Roman arches. Daniele Barbaro himself was on the main balcony on the second floor, and when he saw Trissino and Palladio, he waved in large, sweeping gestures of welcome. They could hear a chorus of dogs as well, which always seemed to surround the barrel-chested Daniele.

A flag popped in the breeze. It featured a red circle on a white background, the emblem of the Barbaro family.

Trissino said, "They say that in the twelfth century, Marco Barbaro had been in a naval battle with a band of Moorish barbarians. He needed to mark his ship, so he cut off the hand of one of the fallen Moors. Using the bloody stump, he drew a circle on a turban and hoisted it up for all to see." He stepped out of the gondolier, leaving Palladio with that vivid image.

They entered the lower floor of the palazzo and into an active warehouse. Men were carrying sacks of salt, bundles of wheat, and bolts of silk in brilliant reds, blues, and golds. Shouting, lifting, and grunting men were in constant motion. After the piercing sunlight of the day, the place was dark, cavernous, and shot through with streams of lights from the open windows.

Suddenly, they were surrounded by five dogs who snuffled and sniffed at their pant legs. Daniele was near. He swept in and the men made room for him, changing their routes of work to accommodate him. He hugged Trissino and Palladio and took them upstairs via a unique staircase that crisscrossed with another staircase. Daniele explained that this double staircase allowed the family and the servants to interact only when they wanted to. As they came out on the second floor, and both staircases met, Palladio marveled at this invention that reflected both privacy and logistical usefulness.

The piano nobile was as quiet as the first floor had been

loud. Daniele led them into a room with high ceilings. Paintings and tapestries covered every wall and spread across the domed ceiling. Stucco relief separated the works of art with garlands, florets, and putti. Gilt-edged frames and gold silk curtains added a layer of richness and wealth to the overall feeling of the room. The dogs settled down on the kilim carpets that covered the marble mosaic floor. Daniele gestured for them to sit and offered them Valpolicella wine, Tuscan grapes, and a wedge of fontina cheese. He said the Lord's Prayer and then they ate. Palladio realized they had eaten nothing since the quick breakfast before dawn and he had to restrain himself from wolfing the cheese down in one gulp.

After they finished, Daniele showed them to their bedrooms. A soiree was planned that evening, so he insisted that they rest and take an afternoon *riposo*. Palladio's bedroom was smaller than Trissino's, of course, but it was sumptuous in its own way. Daniele called it the Oriental Room and it was well named, for it featured paintings of people from the Orient and their gods. The bed was made of a dark wood that Palladio did not recognize. The bedstead featured snakes and wreaths winding around the bed, and for a moment, Palladio doubted that he would be able to sleep in such a tangle of flora and fauna. The minute his head hit the pillows, however, he was asleep.

That night, Trissino and Palladio attended the soiree that Daniele's brother, Marcantonio, had arranged. It took place in the main room that Trissino and Palladio had seen earlier. As they entered, Trissino reconnected with old friends and introduced Palladio as the next great architect. Each time he did,

Palladio blushed, starting at his ears. These events tended to run long with the men finding various activities to while away the hours. Some read books, some drew, and a few occasionally sang.

Trissino and Palladio were engaged in an intense debate about battle strategies. They enjoyed imagining the topography—the hills that hemmed them in, the rivers that could be used as a potential for escape. This time, they were steeped in imagining the Battle of Cannae in 216 B.C. It had been a disaster for the Roman Empire and 90,000 men had died when Hannibal had used the double-envelopment technique on the hapless Romans. Trissino had commandeered two salt cellars, a plate of prosciutto, melons, strawberries, cheese, olives, and grapes to act as armies, trees, hills, rivers, and cliffs. The entire table was a battleground.

They hadn't noticed that an entertainer was setting up a small chair and a music stand. When the room hushed, they both looked up to see a vivid woman in a blood-red dress seated and holding a lute in her arms. She was dark-haired and red-lipped and the smile that she spread around the room seemed meant for each individual man. Daniele introduced her as Madonna Bellina.

When she began to sing, the room ceased to exist, for reality was erased from the very first note. She sang and played her original compositions as though she were an angel incarnate. This woman did the impossible: She looked into the eyes of each man and sang directly to him, making him understand that the song was a special gift written especially for him. Palladio stopped breathing. Or so he thought when the last notes finally faded away and he found himself taking in a huge gulp of air. The applause was thunderous and the men leapt to their feet in a spontaneous gesture of appreciation.

She sat sipping water from a crystal glass while Marcantonio leaned over her protectively and whispered in her ear. She was no ordinary musician, but one that had God's hand placed upon her head. Palladio thought about art and grace and God, and hoped that he, too, would one day be regarded as such an artist.

Marcantonio announced that she would perform a few more songs before taking her leave. Palladio and Trissino noted a few men clumped together in the corner of the room. They were not smiling, but instead glowered at the room and at Madonna Bellina in particular.

Trissino crossed the room and conversed with them. Although Palladio could not quite decipher what was being said, voices were being raised and he saw Trissino gesturing angrily, uncharacteristically upset. Just as Palladio stood to help his friend, the men stomped out of the room. Trissino came back to Palladio and insisted he return to his seat.

"What was that about?" Palladio inquired of Trissino.

"They didn't like the fact that she's a Jew," whispered Trissino.

At that moment, Marcantonio announced that Signorina Bellina would sing an encore. The remaining men quickly took seats. As she began the last song, Palladio couldn't help but hear a change in the music. Somehow it was deeper, much sadder than the first set of songs. *The intervals were designed to make one cry*, he thought. As she strummed the lute, the music cascaded lovingly and sadly, winding its way through his heart.

Palladio was not surprised to see a single tear wind its way down Trissino's cheek. He thought about how dismal a life without art or music or theater would be. How people can silence a voice or the strings on a lute with one word.

When the song was over, Trissino and Palladio joined a group of adoring listeners. They complimented her and put gold coins in a small cup at her feet. She was gracious and kind, with a laugh that was as musical as her song. She sent them all away feeling as though mankind, and in particular womankind, was something to be treasured. Marcantonio had reserved a fine room for her facing the canal, and soon after, she retired to it with a small wave of her hand.

When the rest of the visitors had at last gone home, the two Barbaro brothers, Trissino, and Palladio sat nursing a last glass of Spanish sherry. Marcantonio was so angry he could not sit still. He paced back and forth in anger.

"I have broken the law tonight. Do you know that? And what is my crime? I am housing a Jew. They have locked the gates to the Jewish quarter and neither heaven nor hell can open them again until noon tomorrow. Can you imagine?" He smiled painfully. "That woman may be a Jew, but she is more jewel than Jew to me." He smiled slightly at his own small joke but his face was mottled and pinched and his hands were fists.

Daniele laid a cautionary hand upon his leg, which he brushed off. Palladio knew nothing of this issue, and Marcantonio launched into a tirade asking questions that had no answers.

Unbeknownst to either Trissino or Palladio, Marcantonio had been pushing hard for the council to accept Solomon of Udine, a skilled arbitrator, diplomat, and negotiator as the ambassador to Turkey. All of the council agreed that Solomon was a paragon of virtues, but they had one small problem that reared up as insurmountable: He was Jewish. Marcantonio was tugging so violently on his own beard that Palladio was afraid he would rip it out. Finally, his energy spent, he collapsed on the lemon-colored brocaded couch and absentmindedly stroked one of the silken leaves in the fabric as he shook his head in frustration.

He had been one of only a handful of advocates who had stood up in the council and argued for Solomon's appointment. With two thousand men arguing over a million and one issues, it was difficult to get a decision on any one thing and movement was slow.

Eventually, Marcantonio bade the three men goodnight and plodded from the room, his shoulders slumped.

Trissino, Daniele, and Palladio were overcome with *ennui*, a French term that Palladio had only recently learned. They were so overcome with lethargy and a world-wise weariness that they sat together, none saying a word, for almost an hour. Finally, Trissino murmured something about a meeting with Hypnos and slipped from the room. Daniele soon followed.

Palladio remained, drained by the thought that the world was filled with insurmountable obstacles that could not be overcome. He envisioned a series of spiky trees, growing so close together that no man could slip between them. At last he sighed, pulling himself out of the chair he had occupied for hours. He would go to bed in the snake-bound bed and wake up to a new day.

The remainder of the visit consisted of a string of meetings, parties, soirees, card games, concerts, and strolls. During each event, Palladio felt as though he knew just a little more about the watery city. One day, they were strolling down the Fondamenta della Misericordia in the northern part of the city, away from the Grand Canal and the Doge's Palace. They had turned up the small Calle Forno, one of the pedestrian thoroughfares that was scarcely wide enough for two men to traverse shoulder to shoulder, when they came upon a barricade with a soldier alertly patrolling in front of it.

The soldier said one word when Trissino's eyebrows raised in confusion: "Plague." The word sent shivers of fear into Palladio. The plague reared its ugly head from time to time and the city responded with a furious speed. If there was even a whiff of disease, two people who had been struck down with a cold, or a child who had not been seen for days, it triggered swift action. Barricades were thrown up, soldiers were dispatched. It was better to be safe than sorry.

Trissino and Palladio did not waste breath arguing and turned back the way they came. It did not do to mess with the plague.

After several weeks, it was time to return to Vicenza. Trissino needed to attend to his palazzo, his private school, and his various businesses that kept food on the table.

However, they would have to run one other errand before departing Venice. They needed to visit Jacopo Sansovino, a colleague who had suffered a loss of his own. He was an able architect who had been given the important responsibility of building the library that would house the collection of the manuscripts given to Venice by Cardinal Bessarion in 1468. The doge realized that the collection was languishing and he wanted a prestigious building near his palace that he could visit at his leisure. Sansovino had been the selected architect and all had gone well for eight years.

But just six months ago, the reading room vaults had collapsed. Four workers had been injured and one was killed. This was a disaster for any architect. If people lost faith that your building was safe, you might as well become a pig farmer. Which might have been better for poor Sansovino because instead of playing with pigs, he was in prison.

The prison smelled of urine, feces, and the dankness of mold. Men cried out, snored, and talked in their sleep. When Trissino and Palladio entered and saw the guard, he immediately guessed why they were there. Well-dressed people seldom visited anyone other than Sansovino. The guard led them down a dark stone hallway and stopped in front of a cell lit with four candles.

Sansovino brightened when he saw them and gestured toward his lit tapers. "A luxury. I'm sorry I haven't anything to offer. No bread, no wine, not even a little Asagio cheese," he said with a thin smile.

He bade the jailor get stools for his guests, which they sat on gratefully.

Sansovino began speaking. It was as though a dike had been released. He told them all about what had happened.

"It was frost. I told them it was too cold, but they would not listen. They were wearing gloves and hats and scarves, and still, they would not listen. Their brains were frozen. That is the only explanation."

He grabbed the cell bars, his knuckles turning white. He went on to describe that against his advice, they installed the concrete vault. Even when there was frost on the ground and you could see one's breath. It was idiocy, insanity. And there he was. In prison.

Palladio did not know what to say. As far as he knew, this was an unheard-of response to the failure of a building. He did not know whether it was truly Sansovino's fault, bad luck, or the hand of God. But the man who stood before him was broken. That could clearly be seen. He did not know Sansovino well. He had often been Palladio's competitor and thus he was a kind of professional enemy. On the other hand, he held no true enmity for the man and he had suffered the worst tragedy besides losing a child. He had lost the faith of others.

Trissino patted Sansovino's hand. "I hear that many friends have come to visit you. Titian, and one of the ambassadors of Emperor Charles V . . . and that *writer* Pietro Aretino."

Palladio heard the dismissal in Trissino's voice, for Aretino was, in anyone's book, a scoundrel. People were terrified of him—and furious, too. He had been booted out of Rome for making his living writing scathing satires that named real people. One would think that he would droop his head in shame, but instead, he traveled to Venice. People were so afraid they would be a character in his next lampoon, they drowned him in gifts. He lived on the Grand Canal in style and became friends with the mighty who were afraid to fall.

Sansovino stroked the two panels of white beard that ran down either side of his face and smiled. "When in prison, even Pietro."

Trissino and Palladio promised that they, too, would do what they could to see that he was released from prison, for they knew that God could easily have chosen them instead. As a parting gift, they gave him several loaves of rye bread, three wheels of cheese, and some strawberries. He immediately popped a berry in his mouth and a thin grin appeared under his scraggly, unkempt beard.

Trissino looked at him with genuine warmth. "Goodbye, Sansovino. May you soon find yourself free," he said as he and Palladio departed, and they both felt a kind of shame that they were free to leave while Sansovino was not.

As they exited the prison, they were both downhearted. They passed by the rotting hull of a ship that had landed on the shore, and they sat for a moment and looked at the shape of the hull. Palladio remarked that it would make a beautiful shape for a ceiling and how similar it was to the vaults in the baths they had seen.

Trissino's face brightened. This was the kind of thinking that he appreciated from Palladio. He could see a block of granite and turn it into a man. Or look at a rotting hull and turn it into a beautiful ceiling. In this way, he had the eye of a true artist, for he could see what others could not.

Chapter Sixteen

1547: THE SHADOW AND THE LIGHT

For Trissino, his son Guilio, so unlike Palladio, was like a chronic disease—one that would keep coming back time and time again to torture him. The year had been particularly bad for Trissino. He spent much of the year in bed while doctors came to his bedside and clicked their tongues. That winter had been the coldest that Trissino remembered, so he spent time thinking about the yellow warmth of summer.

It was Christmas Eve, and he was remembering one special summer evening when the temperature was just a few degrees warmer than his skin, and dusk had fallen so slowly and carefully upon his shoulders that he had not noticed it until he could no longer see the poem in front of him. He was lost in that memory when the door to his bedroom burst open and Guilio stood there, the white robes of the church still in motion.

Guilio's face had solidified into a mask of cruelty, and when he smiled at his father, Trissino knew that evil had found a face.

Guilio, brandishing an official document, a red seal upon its creamy cover, sneered at his father and claimed Trissino's house for his own. Backed by a tribunal, the judgment could not be countered. Trissino shrank into the covers, pulling the sheets to his chest, but Guilio grabbed them and yanked them from his father's body, demanding that he leave the house, *his* house, immediately.

Trissino could do nothing but obey. He fled out into the night wearing only his nightwear. His servants led him to the residence of a friend who could house him only as long as he could evade Guilio's spies. Trissino was forced out of his house, out of his life.

When Palladio heard about this, he was at home, working on his book. Allegradonna came to him with a letter in hand that Trissino had sent. Palladio's first instinct was to drop all of his projects, to rush to Venice to be by Trissino's side. But that was not possible. There was no money for such a journey. As was often the case, Palladio cursed the fact that although he lived a rich life full of poetry, philosophy and art, that richness rarely included money.

Trissino was not only his friend. He was the reason for all of his professional success. Without Trissino's patronage and support, he would probably be still cutting stones for others. And he also knew, deep down in his heart, that part of the reason that he and Trissino were so close was due to the failure of Trissino's own son. Much to Trissino's shame and grief, Guilio was a cruel, vile man whose only understanding of family was how it could benefit him.

The very next day, Leonida and Orazio released a pig into the house. It ran squealing throughout the rooms, careening up the stairs and bumping into tables, which turned over. Everything that was upon them crashed and broke upon the wooden floor. Allegradonna was yelling and screaming and hitting the pig with her broom. It took all of Palladio's strength to resist cuffing both of his sons. But when everyone had calmed down and he saw them both asleep in bed, he thought of Trissino's son. He sent an ardent prayer to God: *May I never have a son like Trissino's.* He kissed them both on the tops of their dark heads with the prayer fresh in his thoughts.

Palladio and Allegradonna set out to meet Lady Poiana and her husband, the chevalier Bonifacio Poiana, at the site of the Poianas' new villa. They had rented a small two-wheeled cart that their horse, Ragazzina, could easily pull. They made a day of it and Allegradonna packed a basket with chianti, mozzarella, a large loaf of rye, and a jar of Bella di Cerignola black olives.

Leonida, Orazio, and Zenobia had been left at home because of an unforeseen incident. The day before, they had taken it upon themselves to run away from home. Palladio was fairly certain that the idea had been Leonida's, for he took every chance he could to disrupt the peace of their home and involve his brothers and sisters if possible. Orazio was the reader in the family, innocent and thoughtful, but he worshipped his older brother and was often caught up in the vortex of Leonida's complicated plots.

The three had set off to the south, each with a roll of bread tied up in a knot. They had managed to get miles from town when they decided to take their shoes off and cool their feet in a nearby stream. Seeing Zenobia's shoes on the bank, Leonida persuaded Orazio to join him in hiding them in the hills that cast a shadow above them.

When Zenobia had turned to put her shoes back on, Leonida had fallen on the ground with laughter and told her to go find them. Orazio was already feeling guilty about it and tried to find them for her, but they were lost somewhere in the intricacies of the woods. Leonida claimed he knew exactly where they were and he would tell Zenobia if she was willing to do his laundry for a month.

Zenobia glared at Leonida, turned, and began walking. She would walk. And walk she did, with the boys dragging behind her. By the time they arrived home, the bread was long eaten, the night had fallen, and Zenobia's feet were in ribbons. Although all three begged to come on this rare journey, they all stayed at home. Leonida and Orazio were being punished and Zenobia remained in bed with bandages around her feet. Marcantonio and Silla had thumbed their noses at their siblings and jumped into the cart.

Marcantonio was eager to explore the countryside, since he rarely had the opportunity. He was an adventurous child, a solid boy with a good heart, and he often brought home lost cats and dogs, which they struggled to feed. He was already in an apprenticeship in a design studio, so this was a rare opportunity for him. Silla also came, enticed by a picnic.

Allegradonna didn't want to admit it, but it was a relief to have only two children to keep track of. With only two, she could afford to stare off at the hills or up at the brilliant sky. It was a calming experience and her heart welcomed this moment of peace.

Located in a countryside of rolling hills, stands of poplars, and inviting fishing ponds, the site was twenty miles south of Vicenza and would take most of the day to reach. But for Palladio, there was nothing like standing in the actual site. He would close his eyes and taste the wind, kneel and feel the texture of the dirt. He would know, deep inside, where the building should begin and end.

He was eager to talk to Lady Poiana and Bonifacio for they both carried with them an easy approach to life. He had known Lady Poiana since the days of early courtship with Allegradonna and he had met and admired Bonifacio at Trissino's house. Many of the men he now crossed paths with had received land and money from their grateful patrons for their actions in various wars. These men, eager to shed themselves of all things that stank of death, wanted to surround themselves with the beauty of nature and art. Palladio enjoyed spending time with many of them, as he found that the men who had returned from fields of battle often were the greatest lovers of life and knew how to live theirs well.

As for her part, Allegradonna would be glad to catch up with her mistress, whom she had not seen in years.

Late in the day, they turned off from the main road and took the lane that led to the family's existing farmhouse and tower.

The one-hundred-year-old farmhouse was not much more than a barn, but Bonifacio and his wife greeted them at the door as though they were already in the villa that would soon be theirs.

They talked late into the night. Silla and Marcantonio had long ago been put to bed. Palladio already had so many ideas about the proposed building that they spun in his head. He envisioned a main room with a barrel ceiling, something that he had seen in the Roman baths. Perhaps a circular arch above the doorway with recessed oculi. Bonifacio cautioned him that their money was not grand, that they wanted something statuesque but dignified. A place he could age well in, as he put it. Palladio listened carefully, a talent he had refined since his early days with the mean-spirited Cavazza.

He suggested a broken base cornice in the facade; it would be cheaper and it would echo the outside walls of the Baths of Diocletian in Rome. This kind of thinking delighted Bonifacio and Lady Poiana. They could save money and the design would not be compromised.

Allegradonna listened to the back-and-forth between her talented husband and the couple whose dreams were being built in the air. She never tired of watching how Palladio thought, for his mind never seemed to see impediments, only problems that could be solved.

His mind was like water, always seeking new paths. If not this, then that. She had never seen him stymied for long and it was the fluidity of his thinking that had saved him time and time again. He would create something affordable and beautiful for her lady and husband. They would avoid costly stone, but instead build it out of rendered brick and molded terracotta. They would stucco it so it had the magnificence of stone. It would feature clean lines and restricted statuary so the beauty of the facade would read with clarity. By the time they finally went to bed, a building had taken shape.

Chapter Seventeen

1549: TRANSFORMATION OF THE BASILICA

Palladio was worried about his friend. Trissino had always been somewhere in the background, and even when Palladio could not see him, he could sense his political and social presence smoothing the way toward bigger and ever more prestigious opportunities. For the past six months, however, there had been a void that Palladio felt almost immediately.

He had heard that Trissino was now living in a comfortable house in Venice not far from the Grand Canal, but he was not as active as in the past. Palladio hoped Trissino would travel to Vicenza soon, for he missed him not only as a friend, but also as a political force to be reckoned with. Nothing less than the Palazzo della Ragione was at stake.

The race for who would get to design the palazzo was a crowded one, with many architects, young and old, vying for the honor. Palladio needed Trissino more than ever, but for the last month, he had not been at home and no one seemed to know where he had disappeared to. Palladio was worried. It was not like his friend to vanish for so long.

At times, the Palazzo della Ragione seemed as though it were cursed. Multiple buildings had preceded the existing palazzo, and by the time Palladio came along, they had been incorporated under one roof. In 1481, the city architect Tommaso Formenton began working within its Roman-style vaults to shore up the building, for it was becoming a danger to anyone who came near it, much less the people who worked within it. It was in 1496 that the southwest corner had collapsed, undoing most of the work that had taken place under Formenton.

This was a wake-up call to the public magistrates who kept offices there. They envisioned a terrible sunny afternoon when they would feel the floor tremble and then be buried under rubble, never to see a sunny day again. Something had to be done.

But as is true in most municipal affairs, they argued bitterly over how to solve the problem. For forty years, they had debated and entertained a variety of possible plans, schemes, and ideas that poured from anyone who cared to add their opinion. Spavento, Scarpagnino, Sansovino, Serlio, and Sanmicheli all offered up a variety of ways to solve this rapidly crumbling building set in the center of Vicenza. Romano, who came along in 1542, joked that he should get the job since he was the first architect whose name did not start with "S."

Palladio had also added his plans to the pile, but it wasn't until an ill-looking Trissino reappeared and plied his magic that he could get any traction. The horse race included so many skilled architects and the situation had gone on for so long that perhaps it simply needed one man who knew the players and could manipulate the decision. Or perhaps they were all just worn out. Whatever the true reason, in 1546, they provisionally accepted plans from the thirty-eight-year-old Palladio as long as he partnered with his former boss, the now-ancient Giovanni da Porlezza.

Palladio had grown up professionally under Giovanni's eye and he knew the man from front to back. Now, when Giovanni entered a room, Palladio was the first to offer him a chair, for he was quite elderly and suffered from both gout and a crippling disease that made it hard for him to stand for long. Giovanni, in turn, adored and respected Palladio, and when they worked together on the palazzo drawings, he would often fade away into reminiscing about his youth, allowing Palladio to draw up the plans as he wished.

Allegradonna was ecstatic, as financial worries had been her constant companion. Although Palladio was a brilliant man, money did not follow him easily and it was as though he played a game of hide and seek with it. She hoped that with this opportunity would come a great sum of money. She kissed Palladio mightily when she heard the news and the children bubbled around him. *Perhaps new toys would be in order*, they thought, and shrieked when Palladio and Allegradonna began dancing together in the kitchen.

But cities are like turtles leisurely sunning themselves on a log, and so three long years passed with Palladio and Giovanni presenting a series of plans that the committee pored over. Finally, one cloudy day in February, they once again met with the magistrates, who were in a cranky mood. The delights of Christmas were over and they were stuck inside with their families who were too loud and too excited and took up too much space.

One of the members of the magistrate began complaining. Plans were difficult to understand. They were flat and one couldn't truly get a sense of what they would actually look like. Couldn't these two architects build a little something— say, a life-sized arch—so the magistrates could see the real-world effect?

Palladio and Giovanni exchanged covert glances. What more could they do? They had given their time, their energy, and their creative thinking to a project that was still not confirmed. A life-sized arch was better than giving the magistrates their blood—which was what they were beginning to think these men wanted.

Palladio was standing back, peering at the life-sized model of the proposed arch. The sun was hot and high outside, and through the open door, Palladio watched as a dusty black dog moved out of the sun and into the shade. Trissino appeared in his customary black suit, looking a little like the black dog. Palladio was going to make a joke until he looked at his friend's face and knew immediately that something was wrong.

Giovanni was dead. He had died in his sleep. When the servant had gone to wake him, he was cold and stiff and already meeting God. Palladio shook his head slowly and recalled the last time he had seen his friend and mentor. Just a few days ago, Giovanni had come to visit and had seated himself a good distance from the half-finished arch so as to see it in its entirety. He had critiqued the color a bit, saying it was a shade too dark, and then offered up a pocket full of grapes which, when he brought them out, had been squished to a pulp. They had laughed together and Palladio had taken the grapes from him and fed them to the dog. That was his last memory of the man.

Giovanni di Giacomo da Porlezza, for that was his formal name, was buried in the cemetery in the northern part of the city. The people who attended the funeral represented a cross section of Vicenzan society, including not only the workmen who had brought Giovanni's designs to life, but also the patrons who had paid for them. Giovanni's small, wizened wife was there, and it was clear she welcomed her two strong sons, who supported her as she walked along. She stopped as they passed by Palladio.

"So, you are Palladio," she said in a thin voice, for in all of those years, they had never had the occasion to meet. "Giovanni told me so many wonderful things about you. He said you were a *persona onesta e rispettabile*, an honorable person that one could respect." Then she lowered her voice. "And he also said you were an imp as a young man!" She laughed a little, pressed his hand, and then continued to the gravesite.

Palladio thought back to the early days. Yes, there had been a few moments of impishness. He remembered one sunny day in April, a year after starting his apprenticeship, when he had taped a drawing of a fish onto the back of poor unsuspecting Giovanni.

Palladio had been so skilled at taping it on that when the rest of the boys and Giovanni himself started asking if anyone had seen April's "fish," the never suspected that it was actually him. They had let him look around with the rest of them until Palladio finally revealed that Giovanni was the fish and that Palladio had been the one who had affixed it to his back. Giovanni's response was to swell up, and for a moment Palladio had flashed back to the horrors of his former master. But then Giovanni let loose with a bray of laughter that was so loud, Palladio thought the granite in front of him would crack.

Giovanni had been a wonderful and patient master, a person who had taught Palladio so much about life and about work— from the small details of how to coax a shape from the rigid confines of a piece of granite to how to reward a worker for going over and beyond the confines of his job. He would be sorely missed.

Girolamo Chiericati and Gianalvise Valmarana were sitting at Trissino's massive wooden table when Palladio walked in. Chiericati was in a jovial mood; rumor had it that his wife had just given birth to his third son. He was, by all accounts, a family man, proud of his family of six, running his household with a tilt of his head. Chiericati had seen death and now he embraced life. His dark beard waggled as he bent his head toward Gianalvise, sharing some sort of singular secret.

Gianalvise tugged at his belt and waved at Palladio to take a seat. Trissino entered with an armful of architectural plans and drawings. It took Palladio a moment to realize they were his own. The plans represented many days and nights of challenging work. For weeks Palladio had struggled, and at times he had been tempted to march over to the town council and tell them that what they wanted was idiotic.

Trissino spread the drawings out on the table and weighted three corners down with various tableware. The fourth corner curled up coquettishly and Chiericati settled that by laying down a heavy dagger that he pulled from his voluminous robes.

By the end of the afternoon, it was done. Palladio had signed the papers and he was now officially Vicenza's architect. This would mean that in addition to redesigning the palazzo, he would be responsible for overseeing the designs of the rest of the city. He would work with other architects so the city would maintain a unified architectural narrative. He wished that Giovanni had lived to see this day. It had been a long time coming.

Palladio remembered the day that his thoughts had solidified. He had stood in the main gallery of the Palazzo della Ragione and stared up at the cavernous ceiling. Palladio envisioned Noah building his ark, staring down into the bottom of his boat before the animals had been loaded in. The ceiling looked as though someone had built the curving bottom of the ark and then, before bothering to complete the deck, had hoisted it aloft, turned it upside down, and fastened it into place. Large round windows interrupted the sides periodically, sending faint sunlight into the room. The room was perfect for large gatherings and art exhibitions. This would be preserved, of course. At the moment it was a rich, dark mahogany brown. Palladio wondered what it would look like if he painted it white. Perhaps less like a boat and more like a church. The patrons, however, had said nothing about the interior and Palladio assumed they would kick up a fuss if he played too much with the inside.

The main issue at hand was how to stabilize the interior and emphasize the grandiosity of the building. The patrons had requested that he add a serliana, a series of repeated regular arches with rectangular openings on each side. It seemed impossible to match the existing architecture with a new layer of arches so that they would have any kind of integral harmony. He had tried designing a smaller arch at the ends with two smaller arches in the center, but all of the previous designs had drawn the eye to those arches and they had stood out like the proverbial sore thumbs.

The problem was that the buildings inside had grown organically, rather more like trees than rocks, and over time several buildings had become one. This led to an interesting design challenge. How could he design a loggia, a space made up of a running series of regular arches, that would match the irregular openings of the existing building? Palladio thoughtfully descended the stairs and then walked around the eyesore of a building.

The southwest corner was surrounded by scaffolding and tarps, a weak attempt at keeping the building up and the weather out. The lower floor of the building contained shops: a shoemaker, a millinery, and a jewelry store. They did a brisk business even though the building looked like a neglected child. Although the structure was a hodgepodge, it made a certain sense. If Palladio did his job correctly, he could make the building function as a whole and be perceived as solid, with one design uniting the entire structure.

With sudden inspiration, Palladio reasoned that rules were made to be broken. If he cheated each opening, he could make them seem regular but actually match the interior hallways. It would be a matter of math. Few people casually strolling down the square would realize that the serliana was actually a series of subtly mismatched openings. He repressed a yell of triumph and satisfied his urge with a small dance executed only by his feet.

Palladio thought again about the lofted boat-like ceiling and related it to the groin ceilings of the Baths of Agrippa. He and Trissino had visited these baths on his first visit to Rome. He recalled seeing the partial remains of groin ceilings, the double-vaulted arches featuring two barrel vaults together. These vaults, while more complex to build than the simpler barrel vaults, would be perfect for this project. These arches were strong, thrusting most of the weight through the four corners. They were expansive in feeling, and the light tended to bounce around within them rather than being crushed by the parallel walls of the barrel vaults. If he used groin ceilings in the loggia, it would echo the larger interior ceiling and add light and drama.

Palladio looked around him. A hundred years from now, people would do what they were doing now—selling wares; leading their dogs up and down, competing for which one was tougher and which more beautiful; young people flirting cautiously; old people rotating with the sun like oversized sunflowers. And in the midst of all of this human activity would be a building that embraced it all: the flirting, the competing, the various natures of man.

From that moment forward, Palladio would refer to this new building—one that would rise like a phoenix—as the Basilica. It would rival other equally prestigious buildings such as the basilicas he had measured in Rome. . . .

Palladio shook himself out of his reverie and came back to the present. He was the city's new architect! He bid the men goodbye and rushed home to tell the very patient Allegradonna the news. Five gold *scudi* per month!

For once, Allegradonna had no words to say. Her chin dropped and silence poured out. Palladio took her in his arms and buried his face in her shoulder. She had borne much. She had been forced to be clever with a single chicken, stretching it to feed her own brood of five chicks. She had been masterful at making the small earnings that Palladio had brought home cover the rent for their meager flat and enough food to feed their family. Five gold *scudi* meant that they would be able to have cheese as well as bread, wine as well as water. It would be a whole new world for them.

Chapter Eighteen

Palladio dismounted from Ragazzina and immediately a wine cart almost ran over him. Fishmongers, barrel makers, bakers, furniture makers, and cobblers had all set up shop, for this was market day. The Retrone and the Bacchiglione Rivers, meeting nearby, were filled with gondolas, dories, barges, skiffs, and punts, all vying for dock space.

The air was as crowded as the rivers, for everyone was trying to outshout the rest. The idea of building a peaceful home for Count Girolamo Chiericati at this site seemed impossible. And at least once, if not twice a year, it flooded. The area in front of the proposed site, often called l'Isola ("the Island"), was defined by the two rivers that came together at that point.

The smell of cattle assailed Palladio's nose. He clamped a cloth over his face to temper the aggressive stink of urine and cow dung. The mooing of terrified animals merged with shouts from the cattle dealers who, with foreign gestures, somehow managed to communicate and seal deals. Next to the cattle pens, a similar cacophony was occurring, with barking sellers and eager buyers. There was a small area of relative peace—what could be thought of as the fallen forest, as people were vying for thick boards of maple, oak, walnut, pine, chestnut, beech, and poplar, which were laid end to end in stacks as tall as a man. The buyers scurried over the stacks of lumber like squirrels, pointing out the knots and ax marks that marred the rough yet elegant surfaces.

Palladio could not imagine how he could design a quiet home for Chiericati in this place of noise, dust, and offensive smells. But he owed a lot to this man. Chiericati, along with Trissino, had been a loud and insistent voice of support for Palladio when the Basilica's architect was being chosen.

Once, when he and Trissino had been dining al fresco in Trissino's open arbor, Trissino told him that Chiericati had appreciated the friendly demeanor that Palladio seemed to carry with him every day. It was common knowledge that Chiericati had been worn down by a series of bloody military campaigns. Because of this heavy history, he craved a lightness of spirit, and Palladio, with his easy manner and ready smile, was a tonic. Palladio made him feel that life was not all violence, severed limbs, and tyranny. Chiericati also felt that the drawings reflected imagination and a strength of design that he had not seen in the other proposals. And once he made a decision about a man, he never changed it.

Palladio was bumped from his reverie by the sound of a mongrel dog who was growling at a pair of yoked oxen. One ox lowered his head and would have charged if he had not been restrained by the heavy wooden beam that lay upon his thick neck. The driver kicked the dog, who whimpered and retreated. Palladio sighed. How could this possibly work?

He met with Chiericati in the house that he shared with his brothers. Chiericati resembled the desk at which he sat; even though he was over fifty, his body was as hard as oak and seemed built of right angles. The wars had driven into him a certain spartan, austere approach to life, yet Palladio could see how he leaned toward the light like a starved sapling. When Palladio entered the room, he smiled as though it hurt and extended his hand in greeting. Palladio carried the first drafts of his proposed building under his arm.

Chiericati was a determined man and nothing could shake his belief that building on this busy municipal spot was a wonderful idea. He had already succeeded in convincing the city planners to allow him to tear down three secondary buildings that his family owned on the site. The trouble was that any building of any size would require the depth of the current site to be increased, and that extra land was owned and operated by the city. He mentioned this to Palladio, who tugged on his beard in thought.

Palladio had a solution. What if Chiericati were to convince the city planners that this structure would add to the beauty and prestige of the city itself? If they would let him push his building out into the municipal land, he would create a sort of arcade for the public; something that would contribute to the comfort and ornamentation of the whole city. He would essentially share his front porch with the citizens of Vicenza.

Chiericati enthusiastically agreed, for most of his time would be spent on the second floor where he could enjoy the river vistas. He could afford to share the lower loggia with the denizens, and besides, he had already been thinking about how to give back to the city that had been so supportive of the Chiericati family.

Palladio uncurled the plans and began to describe his ideas. First and foremost, he would have to raise the building. If he built the first floor even with the ground, the yearly floods would surely destroy all furnishings, tapestries, and rugs and leave a sodden smell that would never disappear. In addition, a raised floor would add an air of grandeur to the palazzo.

Chiericati nodded eagerly, saying, "Go on, go on."

Palladio was interested in experimenting with Tuscan columns. These columns, known for appearing strong and masculine, were thinner than the Doric column and would reflect a certain military air. Then Palladio presented an idea he was the most excited about: a colonnade, a series of columns that would support the loggia, opening the space up visually and psychologically. The building would have three bays in the front facade with the middle bay protruding slightly. It would feature two stacked loggias with Tuscan columns on the first floor and Ionic columns directly above them on the second floor. He proposed a double loggia, one on the first floor and one on the second. Both would run the length of the building.

Chiericati frowned slightly. He drew his blunt index finger

along the plan, insisting that the second-floor loggia not run the length of the building; rather, the center area should be enclosed, allowing him to peer down on the happenings in the area and yet remain hidden. As he expressed his desires, his body seemed to become even more blocky and granite-like.

Palladio looked at the man before him. He realized he had unconsciously designed the building as though personifying Chiericati himself. The desk was like the building, and the building, like Chiericati. The building would feel like this man with his military carriage—straight, bold, imposing.

Palladio consented, for that was how it always was: a back-and-forth between patron and architect, a push and pull that, with luck and God's blessing, eventually resulted in something that emerged from the earth in the form of a building.

Chiericati brought out four gold *scudi*, causing Palladio's eyebrows to raise in surprise. With a flamboyant hand, Chiericati drafted an agreement. These *scudi* would pay Palladio to create the series of plans and drawings necessary before the building could be built.

Palladio swept up the coins and put them quickly in his pocket before Chiericati could change his mind. Allegradonna would be nothing short of thrilled, for keeping food in the pantry was still a constant headache.

Palladio was emboldened to talk about some of the architectural details he thought would fit Chiericati's disposition. He suggested that they include a bucrania motif as a major part of the decorative frieze that would line the building. These carved decorations depicted the heads of oxen. Sometimes these oxen were heads with skin and muscle, but often they were simply skulls that looked down hollowly at the people below. Palladio had used them with great effect on his Basilica. These heads represented sacrifice, for in ancient Rome, oxen had been offered up as sacrifices to gods such as Mars, Jupiter, and Apollo. Chiericati was enthusiastic, for these barren skulls often represented military sacrifice, something he knew only too well.

Together, they discussed the garlands that often hung from the bucranium's horns: fruit or flowers or simple tassels. They considered each in turn and Palladio found in Chiericati a studied logical progression to his thinking. Perhaps simple tassels would suffice? They left the decision open and moved on to the structural details of the interior, discussing them at length far into the night.

When they had finally run out of energy and candlelight, Palladio made his way home through the silent cobblestone streets. His footsteps were loud and echoed back and forth between the buildings. Although it was late and Palladio was immensely tired, he was also ecstatic. Maybe this building could be built. Maybe it could be built in his lifetime. There were many maybes, for he knew that this process was like being a circus dog; there were multiple hoops to jump through. If everything came together—if the city agreed, the family agreed, the money came through, peace reigned, and no unexpected disasters occurred—this building, with its impressive military bearing, would transform the space forever until it was knocked down by fate.

As he approached his small home, tucked between a butcher

and a house owned by the local magistrate, he saw that Allegra-donna had left an oil lamp burning in the window. His heart warmed in anticipation of slipping in under the blue quilt.

Palladio was at his desk, focusing on a line drawing of an intricate vignette. He was struggling to get the leaves exactly right when he heard pounding on the door. He hardly looked up. *Let the servants handle this one*, he thought, for he was just now getting to the central vein that divided the leaf in two.

The servant came into his study accompanied by a messenger who bore terrible news.

Trissino was dead. Dead in his house in Rome.

Palladio carefully laid his pen down. *Trissino dead.* He didn't want to believe it. He should have been there when his benefactor, his friend, died. His mind raced. Was any family there? Was he surrounded by people who loved him? Did the doctors come? Did they try to bleed him? Did they lay leeches upon his chest? Had all that could be done been done? And who had given him his last rites? Not that sodden Cardinal Ricardo, he hoped. No, he hoped it was the priest Eduardo, for he would make sure that Trissino would be escorted from this life to the next with poetry and symmetry. He would give him his last rites, and when he touched him on his brow, it would be with a tenderness and solemnity. If he was conscious, Trissino would have felt that touch and been soothed by it, understanding that he was about to know the greatest mystery and be content.

Palladio lay his forehead down on his desk and felt the

coolness of the wood. A light was gone. He imagined Trissino at the gates of heaven. Saint Peter would joyfully wave him through as though whisking a child through, for there could have been no person better suited for heaven than Trissino.

That night he dreamed that he had been in Rome for Trissino's death. In the dream, Palladio hurried through the archway, for once not bothering to analyze the brickwork. Without pausing, he handed his hat and coat to Trissino's servant, who waited for him in the hall, and hurried to Trissino's bedroom. He opened the door slowly, fearing what he might find. A single candle guttering by Trissino's bedside table made shadows jump and wheel across the walls. They became like demons, warring for Trissino's soul, and Palladio batted at the walls as though they were flies.

He neared the bed with trepidation. For a moment, he remembered another bed, another moment, when his father was near death. Then suddenly his father, as though conjured up by the memory, stood on the other side of the bed, obscured by darkness. His head was cocked down, staring at Trissino. And in the dream this was natural, for although Trissino was not his blood relative, he had acted as a father to him, sheltering him, educating him, caring for his welfare as though Palladio was his own.

Palladio felt his heart turn in his chest for he could not endure yet another death, especially of someone who had single-handedly made such a difference in his life. But he heard the reassuring sound of breath. While there was breath, there was life. Trissino, now seventy-two years of age, seemed to be sleeping . . . until suddenly, as though a knife had sliced through it, the breathing stopped.

Palladio lurched up in bed, gasping as though he also had stopped breathing. He slumped forward, sobbing. His best friend, Gian Giorgio Trissino, was dead.

Chapter Nineteen

1551: VILLA CORNARO

Palladio stood under an ash tree, his drawings spread out before him. The day was fresh after a spring shower, and he breathed deeply, savoring the clean, damp nip in the air. In his mind, the building stood up from his carefully drafted lines and formed a three-dimensional structure. He could see it clearly. It would give the owner, Giorgio Cornaro, a sense of majesty. Perhaps even more importantly, it would overshadow the nearby estate owned by Andrea, his elder brother.

Giorgio rode up on a massive black horse, a *Cavallo Romano della Maremma Laziale*. Palladio knew the exact type of horse because as Giorgio dismounted, he was already informing Palladio about the magnificent animal, who then blew softly into Giorgio's open palm. Giorgio, thirty-seven years old, was rather slight, with a wisp of black hair that kept falling into his eyes. He looked over at his brother's villa. Designed by Michele Sanmicheli, the villa was a stone's throw away from the land that

Giorgio had managed to wring out of the family estate. On the other side of the relatively small plot of land stood a large *barchessa*, a farm building designed by Scamozzi that currently held most of the area's supply of winter wheat. Because Palladio was limited in terms of a usable footprint, his plan was to go in the only direction possible: up.

Giorgio tied his horse to a tree branch and sat down in the shade. He spoke softly about his intended new bride, Elena Contarini. She was sixteen, ready to be wed, the sister of the bishop of Padua. It would be an auspicious match. Not only would she bring a hefty dowry, but she was also a perfect partner for him. She liked horses and dogs, and didn't like his older brother. They were united in wanting a home that would rival her future brother-in-law's fine house.

Palladio was not surprised by this request. The in-fighting and competition rampant in the noble houses of Padua made him glad that he had no siblings of his own. Many wanted to one-up each other with bigger, more magnificent edifices than even they could afford. One of Palladio's secrets to success was his ability to create buildings that looked fit for a king while costing only what an earl could afford.

Together they walked the available parcel. It felt small, hemmed in by the two buildings. Giorgio wiped the sweat from his brow and expressed worry about whether the site could ever work for what he envisioned. Palladio understood. He had met Giorgio's brother Andrea twice and found him to be a swaggering braggart, prone to boasting while drinking so much red wine, he was often found passed out in the streets outside of Il Cuore Lacero (The Tattered Heart), the only tavern that the nearby town of Piombino Dese could claim.

Palladio led Giorgio back to the shade of the tree where his black horse grazed peacefully. He showed Giorgio the drawings and said five words to him: "The only way is up."

Giorgio looked at him, smiled, and then devoured the plans, asking detailed questions and making suggestions. For once, Palladio enjoyed this part of the process. He found Giorgio to be the sort of man who took it upon himself to be educated about a great many things. He wanted to understand the world he lived in, so he made it his business to know a little about everything. He had done his homework and his questions were about structural integrity and materials.

Palladio reassured him. The building would feature a double portico with six Ionic columns on the first floor and six Corinthian columns on the second floor positioned directly over the Ionic columns. On the front facade, the portico would be pushed out so that when he and his young bride stood upon it, they only had to look to the left, to the center, and to the right to see a one-hundred-and-eighty-degree panorama of their acreage. An echoing portico would be on the back side as well, but that one would be flush with the rest of the building.

Twenty-four large structural beams would be laid down on both floors. On top of those beams Palladio would place two layers of planks. The first layer would be placed perpendicular to the beams in order to strengthen the building overall and the second layer would be placed perpendicular to the first layer. A terrazzo floor would be laid upon the last layer to give strength, warmth, and color to the interior.

Palladio made a mental note to personally supervise the making of the terrazzo. He always demanded that unless instructed differently, the terrazzo floors in his buildings would be made of only three things: pulverized brick, rounded river pebbles, and stones. But in the past, he had found a peach pit, chips of a broken china plate, the skull of a lizard, and a child's top.

He would make sure to have Alonzo do this job, for Alonzo was a trustworthy and careful craftsman who specialized in terrazzo flooring. He was a man whose every gesture was calculated to produce works that reflected a certain order, an attention to detail that Palladio respected.

Alonzo and his handpicked crew would begin by applying a four-inch-deep layer of powdered tile and lime. Then each man would don a large cloth bag that he would hang over his shoulder. While the slurry was still wet, they would pull out handfuls of the brick and stone, and with measured gestures similar to a farmer sowing seed, they would sew the slurry with the stone and brick material. Finally, they would take up large, flat boards and press the stone materials flat and smooth. Palladio assured Giorgio that this floor would withstand the harshness of the military boot and the softness of a toddler's tread for five hundred years or more.

After a leisurely repast of rye bread and cheese, they walked the property once more. They talked of many things. Giorgio's villa, like most of the other villas in the area, would do double duty as a family domicile and a working farm. The basement would be a place to make wine and the attic would be a granary. They walked to the edge of a small pond on the property and talked about the intense flavor of venison.

Giorgio had an interesting suggestion. Perhaps tunnels could be built that would connect the pond with the cellar. Not only would they add access to the pond for easy cleaning of the wine casks, but they could also ventilate the basement and freshen the air during the fermentation process. Palladio looked at Giorgio with new respect. This was a fine idea that he would investigate further.

Giorgio began to like this architect, this man who was sincere, well spoken, and at times funny. He gingerly broached the topic of money. Certainly he wanted this building to rival his brother's. He wanted it to be grand. He wanted Elena to be able to walk through the halls with pride. But he also wanted to make sure he could afford it.

They were standing under a willow tree by the pond. Palladio laid a reassuring hand on Giorgio's arm. Like most of the other villas around, Giorgio's villa would appear to be made of stone—imposing and strong—but it would actually be composed of a cheaper material: brick. The brick would be laid so that it would be invisible when covered with intonaco, a stucco-like substance that could be scored to look like any size stone he could desire. By the time he was finished, the building would appear to be stone through and through.

Giorgio once more attempted to push a black strand of hair out of his face. Palladio was tempted to pull his knife out and cut it off. Giorgio wanted to know about the interior. What would it feel like?

Palladio tried to paint a picture that was as clear to Giorgio as it was to him. They sat under the willow tree in close companionship, like a father reading to his child. They faced the space where the building would soon stand.

Palladio began at the front of the house. "To start, you will mount the main stairs and feel as though you are climbing to Mount Olympus. You will stroll between five massive columns through a space that is exactly two and a quarter times the diameter of the columns. You will stride through the portico space until you come to a large wooden door." He took a moment to muse. "Oak, or perhaps walnut." He envisioned the wood, first seeing the doors in walnut, dark and somewhat forbidding, and then lighter, with the pale sunniness of oak. "It will take some effort to push the doors open, for they will be much taller than a man, and in keeping with the theme of height, they will make visitors feel as though they are entering a room of importance and wealth."

Giorgio nodded. This he appreciated.

Palladio continued. "You will be able to see two rooms on your right and on your left, but your attention will be drawn forward toward the main salon. This salon will beckon you with southern windows that will beam in warm shafts of sunlight. It will stun you with high ceilings that will allow you to see the underside of the wooden floor above. Your ancestors will be represented as statuary occupying six niches designed for just that purpose. Four Ionic columns will echo the columns holding up the portico. It will be a room of comfort and symmetry."

Giorgio nodded, his black hair bobbing with the movement.

"And most of all," and here Palladio paused for effect, "all of the rooms will stand in relationship to the others. Two of the side rooms will equal the size of the salon. Although you and your new bride might not know it, you will feel this relationship in your bones."

Giorgio stood and looked out into space, his hand shielding his eyes from the sun. Palladio knew he had succeeded in sharing his vision of the building. This was an ability he was admired for. It was a critical tool in convincing people to take him up on his designs. It took a good and imaginative listener, the time to lay it out correctly, and the perfect setting, usually the site where the building was going to be built.

By the time Giorgio was once more on top of his black stallion, the plan was in motion and ground would be broken within the month. There was no time to lose because his marriage to Elena was imminent. After they were married, they would stay in their Venice home for the next two to three years, or as long as it would take to construct their new house. But as soon as possible, and as soon as the summer heat began, they would want to be in the countryside.

They would bring their tapestries and oil paintings up from Venice until frescoes were added to the building. Their dogs and their horses would join them, and of course the small yellow cat that Elena was known for having with her at all times. They would bring long tapestries for the doorways of each room, for guests and family members would be invited to take up residence to get away from the swampy heat of Venice and admire the new house while doing so. Giorgio would be able to supervise the making of wine and the wheat yields while Elena could supervise the cooking and cleaning, and together they would make the building not only a house and a place of business, but also a home.

As Palladio rode back into town, he mused about the fine houses he had designed and how the people must feel living in them. He compared it to his own rude house, which he rented from an ancient widow who lived next door. Would he ever have a house of his own? Would Allegradonna, a splendid cook, ever have a kitchen of her own? When they made holes in the walls would there ever be a time when those holes would be their holes?

Oh, the house he would design for his family of seven. The children would have a playroom all to themselves. He would have a studio. Allegradonna would have a sewing room where, as she grew old, she could sit in the sun and warm her bones. He shook his head. Although he was a man of imagination, he could not picture ever having the money to afford that.

Palladio was certain that his elegant design for the bridge in Venice would be chosen. He had done some of his best work. The bridge would be made of three parallel streets spanning the

Grand Canal. Shops would thrive on the streets along the sides, meaning they would add taxes for the upkeep of the bridge. He designed a series of arches, a loggia where merchants could meet each other both formally and informally. This area would feature a roof, keeping the rain out so the merchants could meet over tea or wine at their leisure. Three arches would stand within the canal to keep the bridge safe and solid, and statuary would peek from arched niches along the way. Palladio was confident that he would beat out Vignola, who had designed the spectacular Villa Giulia for Pope Julius III; Sansovino; and even the ruffian Michelangelo.

But Palladio had not known about one important requirement. The bridge could not obstruct boat traffic in any way, and three arches were seen as a design with impossible impediments. Only one architect had turned in a single-span design, and that was Antonio da Ponte, a Swiss-born Venetian architect and engineer. He had beat them all out with information that Palladio suspected was kept from the rest of them: The bridge needed to be single span. Da Ponte had figured out a way to repeat the previous wooden bridges that had, over the centuries, burned or fallen down.

When the decision was announced, many knowledgeable men came forward declaring that it was a travesty, a design that would collapse in time. Palladio himself had reservations about how solid this single span could be, but the design was chosen and the building would begin construction within the next few years.

Palladio tried to hide his disappointment and was largely successful—except with Allegradonna. Only she saw how truly dejected he was.

"It would have been so beautiful," he sighed about his rejected design as they walked arm in arm in the Piazza dei Signori. "It would have reflected over the Grand Canal on still nights. It would have been used and enjoyed by hundreds of people a day. It would have been a jewel in the crown of Venice!" Palladio snagged a ball that had bounced near his leg and threw it back to a fluffy white dog, who grabbed it up in his mouth with joy. "It would have meant so much more work," he added sadly, squeezing Allegradonna's arm.

She stopped him, made him turn toward her, and kissed him lightly on the cheek. "There will always be other jewels," she said. "Besides, if it collapses, da Ponte could well find himself in jail, a place that you would not want to be. The officials are foolish, headstrong. When it comes to Venice, you would do well to keep to the church."

Over the years, Palladio had learned to trust Allegradonna's counsel, and this time was no different.

He reasoned that he could make this design live in his book. It would become one of his many "inventions"—buildings that would not be built during his lifetime, but perhaps live a life long after he was gone.

Chapter Twenty

1554: TWO GUIDEBOOKS AND ANOTHER TRIP

Allegradonna was sitting at the kitchen table. Spread in front of her were ledgers, a bottle of ink, and a shallow dish for moistening her fingers. She was flipping rapidly back and forth between ledgers, making calculations as she went. For her, numbers were like candy; she scooped them up by the handful. She enjoyed providing this numerical support to her husband's business and it was a way for her to use her mind beyond calculating the cost of the next meal.

Lately, however, the numbers had jeered at her from the page. Even with Palladio's earnings from the city, money was going out much faster than it was coming in.

Palladio passed by on his way to the bedroom. He stopped when he saw that she was poring over the family ledgers. He hadn't known how bad things were until she shared the ledger with him. They were in trouble. Worse trouble than ever before.

Although he still retained his yearly sum from the city of

Vicenza, business had been slow. Many of his patrons were in an austere mood, for the Holy Roman Emperor Charles V was warring with Henry II of France. In times of war, his patrons rarely thought about new buildings, and he had not received a commission for two years. Occasionally, he had been able to pick up some stone-carving work, but he was no longer a young man and the physical toil of heavy labor had proven difficult.

It was a cloudy, windy, heavy-hearted day. Palladio went up to his drafting table to work on his book, his lifetime endeavor, trying hard not to focus on his recent failures. But like a stubborn horse, all his leaden brain wanted to do was to revisit the scenes of "no." "No, we have chosen someone else," "No, we do not need your services," "No, we aren't interested." It was difficult not to translate those rejections into "You are not of noble birth and therefore you will not receive this commission," "You don't know what you are doing," and worst of all, "Yes, as you suspected, you are an unskilled faker." Palladio sighed and put his pen down. In this frame of mind, no work would get done that day.

He might as well spend time with Zenobia. He grabbed his hiking staff and called for his daughter, who was helping Allegradonna with shelling peas. After a little bit of cajoling and a kiss on Allegradonna's warm brown neck, he was able to liberate Zenobia from her kitchen chores. He suggested that they go and gather grapes. Zenobia squealed in appreciation. She jumped at anything that would get her out of the house and into Vicenza's surrounding fields.

As they wound their way down the curving streets, she

skipped ahead, her peach-colored dress looking like a dancing piece of fruit, her dark hair braided and looped into dangling catenary arches. Soon, they came to a parcel of land whose farmer allowed them to pick his fruit in exchange for Allegradonna's letter-writing skills.

Zenobia found something interesting. She fell to her knees in the dirt and put her nose down close to the ground. Palladio hurried to catch up to her, worried about snakes, spiders, and a poisonous plant, the Italian arum. He had once caught Zenobia with a fistful of its enticing red fruit, ready to pop one experimentally into her mouth, an action that might have killed her. Since then, he had been careful to school her on poisonous plants and on the common viper, a large triangular-headed, fat-bodied snake that was rarely seen in the daytime.

This day, she spied a bright red beetle in the grass. They discussed why it was red, what caused the brilliance of the color (had someone painted it?), and where it might live. Together, they built the beetle's home in their minds. It had small round windows, a mud roof, and a sunny pool in the back where they raised mosquito larvae for dinner.

Most of the day, however, her attention was heavenward and they spent much of their time on their backs, staring at the billowing clouds, where they found a fighting ship, a pig, a goblet, and a lady's fine slipper. Before the day was out, they managed to harvest a sack full of grapes, and Palladio's mind was a little lighter compared to the heavy thoughts of the morning.

After a lean dinner of grapes, bread, and cheese, he sat down at his desk to think. What would bring money through the door?

He racked his brain, and after a while his mind felt like one of Allegradonna's gray cleaning rags. He could think no more.

Allegradonna entered, a card in her hand. She had forgotten to mention that while they were out in the fields, a mysterious embossed letter had arrived. The creamy white letter had a red wax seal on it that included a stamped "S." Palladio's mind scrolled through all of the people he knew whose names began with that initial. The list was lengthy. He opened the letter and a well-trimmed single card fell out. It was from Girolamo da Schio and Chiericati. Palladio did not know Schio personally, but knew that he had recently moved to Vicenza and that he was skilled at fencing, horsemanship, Latin, and drawing. The rumor mill had been working well that week.

The card was an invitation to become a member of a new arts, mathematics, and letters club, the Accademia Olimpica. Palladio's mood shifted slightly. Perhaps this represented a turning point. This was an invitation to become a part of Vicenza's thinking elite.

The next Friday, he and twenty other men gathered at da Porto's home. The piano nobile had been designed with just such a large group in mind and had high ceilings, an expansive floor plan, and a roaring fireplace with a mantle that included carved putti and grape leaves within its oak shelf.

The men were in fine spirits for they were excited about this new gathering. Unlike any other similar group that had been organized before, this one was not arranged around class, but rather around skills. The members were scholars, painters, poets, doctors, philosophers, playwrights, and musicians. Some of Palladio's friends were in the room, and many of the noblemen he had wanted to meet were there as well.

After the men enjoyed a few glasses of wine, the room was cleared of chairs and a rousing fencing match began. Two young men whom Palladio did not know parried, lunged, and recovered. He learned a new term: to *flèche*, which was defined as a sudden explosive attack in which one of the men ran at the other. The round lasted for nine minutes, with the man in the red vest winning after fifteen touches of his rapier. It showed the skill of both parties that neither of them had shed a drop of blood.

Next, a poet who had been traveling through town recited three lyrical poems about death on the battlefield. Once more, Palladio was grateful he had not been swept up into any war, compelled to fight and potentially lose his arm along with his ability to draw.

The rest of the evening was taken up with a lively discussion about the rules and formation of the group. In order to belong, one had to be able to speak and write some Latin. And one needed to have a major skill, which, although generally thought to be in the arts or mathematics, could include horsemanship. One rather bleary-eyed man in a green vest and a feathered hat sitting in front of the fire cheered at this statement. Most were men from all walks of life, but educated in the finer arts, who would be able to contribute to loftier subjects such as the meaning of life, the perfect line, and the most comforting color.

It was well past midnight when they adjourned. As Palladio walked along the street, he marveled at the overhanging balconies and the drooping baskets of pink roses and creeping vines. The summer air had cooled with the setting of the sun and he heard a nightjar trill. He knew the myth about these birds. They were said to suckle goats. He imagined the fat brown bird attempting to get at the she-goat and the goat giving it a swift kick in the head. The vision made Palladio laugh out loud.

He trusted that all would be well, for at heart, he was a man who believed in the will of God and the idea that God loved his children and would provide for them. His fortune would turn around as surely as he could still twirl and spin his daughter in his arms.

Several days after the exhilarating dinner, Palladio was in his room thinking once again about money. What did he have that he could sell? There was no extra furniture, for everything was in use and they only had one chair per family member. They had no extra clothes to sell and certainly no jewelry. What did he have? His mind roamed around his house, discarding one idea and then another. It wasn't until he came back into the very room he was sitting in, the combination bedroom and workroom, that he had a brainstorm. He had his notes from Rome. He could take those notes, improve on them, and then publish them. People would love to know where to go to see what was left of ancient Rome. Followers of history, artists, tourists, all trying to understand what had been before.

He pulled out his voluminous drawings and notes from his trips to Rome and riffled through them with an eye for picking out elements that would be of interest to the casual tourist. As he looked through his papers, an idea came to him. He would make the book pocket-sized so that it could fit easily within one's coat and be close at hand when someone stumbled over a ruin. He would encourage a kind of meandering and give that meandering a form by highlighting four different walks, all starting from the seven main churches of Rome.

He remembered a book that Trissino had carried with him at all times while visiting Rome. This book, called *Le Cose Maravigliose dell'Alma Citta di Roma* (*The Marvels of Rome*), was a popular guide and contained stories and fables that would be of interest to a religious pilgrim. That guidebook joined a long line of *mirabilia urbus Romae* that dated as far back as the days of Pliny the Elder. Palladio's guidebook would carry on this grand tradition, but his book would be focused primarily on the architecture.

His mind rested on that idea for a moment. It would be too bad to limit the book to buildings.

Human behavior, with its traditions and peculiar customs, was too interesting to ignore. When visiting Rome, Palladio had been drawn in by the stories surrounding Roman rituals—for example, how they separated or divorced. Trissino had studied this tradition closely, curious about how to dissolve the institution of marriage, probably due to the instability of his own. In ancient Rome, men could divorce their wives against their will in an act called "repudiation." A husband could repudiate the marriage for a variety of reasons: if his wife was caught talking to the wrong person (a woman of ill repute), leaving the house without a veil, or going to a public show without the husband's permission. Only if both husband and wife agreed would the dissolution be called a divorce. Palladio's book would include these kinds of details—details that would entrance husbands- and wives-to-be.

He would also include funeral rites, for the rituals were elaborate with specifics. For great and wealthy men, the honors due to them went on for days. First, there was a series of oratories. A public square was used for the occasion and men stood up and proclaimed the merits of the dead for all to hear. Second, there was a gladiator-style game with men showing off their battle abilities. (Palladio thought this to be most ironic—the living displaying the highlights of life before the dead.) Then there was a huge banquet with food such as dormice in cream and butter, bream with their fresh eyes still dark (due to aquatic farms), veal, fattened ducks cooked in wine, strawberries, quinces, blackberries, currants, oysters, *juscellum* (a broth made with eggs), saffron, sage, grated bread and eggs, and garum, a fish sauce that was put on everything from breads to egg dishes.

The fourth element of any important funerary rite was to hand out meat to the poor; the more people the family could feed, the more honor the dead had received. Palladio thought that this last honor was the most impressive of all. A splendid humanist gesture. He would publish a book that would allow people to step back in time and, as they wandered the ancient city, imagine what life had been like.

Perhaps he would write two books—one that was focused on the religious buildings and one that focused on the city itself. He would start at the beginning and tell the tale of Romulus and Remus, the twins who had been suckled by wolves.

He drew out a new piece of treasured blank paper and began to write.

Another visit to Rome was needed and Palladio knew the companion he would choose: the erudite Daniele Barbaro. They had been toying with writing a new translation of Vitruvius's *De Architectura*, for both men were sincere in their admiration of the great thinker and designer. If they journeyed to Rome together, they would be saturated in the same environs in which Vitruvius wrote his esteemed book. Their plan was simple: Daniele would edit and translate the text, and Palladio would contribute drawings.

When Palladio made the suggestion to Daniele at one of their many Accademia Olimpica dinners, Daniele immediately poured two glasses of claret and sealed the deal. Daniele was especially keen to go, for he was also an amateur architect and relished the idea of roaming the streets of Rome with Palladio—critiquing the architectural designs as they imagined them, experiencing the regional dishes, and participating in late-night conversations that would cover such topics as the definition of a well-educated man to what was inside of a fish.

After most of the men had departed, Palladio drew Daniele aside and expressed his issues about money. Daniele put his hand on Palladio's shoulder and assured him that he would pay his expenses as well as provide for his family while they were gone. He thought that the book could make money and he promised to travel to Rome after it was finished to tout it to his many friends.

And so they went. The two men bonded over the activity of thinking for pleasure. Their minds were filled with visions of change—how they could change the landscape, change the way that people lived, change the way that animals lived with people, change the way that water was delivered to a house, and, when they were sitting around the fire and the stars were careening overhead, change the very nature of human existence, for their conversations were expansive and sometimes even the heavens were discussed.

Daniele was concerned with aesthetics as a way of life. He and Palladio often found themselves lost in conversations that attempted to define beauty; how one line could make or break a design, how mathematics could be used to create a pleasurable environment, why music was so connected to powerful emotions. They pondered these mysteries and more throughout the night.

Daniele was particularly interested in the "Delian problem," an ancient mathematical problem that involved doubling the volume of a cube. According to an ancient legend, Apollo had asked the Delians, an association of Greek city-states, to double a cube-shaped altar so that they could be rid of one of the many plagues that continued to torture the Greeks. Daniele had tried repeatedly to solve the problem with a simple ruler and compass, but failed. For a brief period of time, Palladio had attempted it as well, but then recognized that the Delian problem would probably take a lifetime to solve. He had problems that were more relevant to him, such as how to make money to feed his family.

Palladio took notes on everything, jotting down each conversation, taking notes on every place he visited. One of his favorite haunts was the Apostolic Library inside the Vatican, which was packed with ancient manuscripts. He could have spent his life there. Sometimes Daniele would have to pry him away, for the stories that the library contained were endlessly interesting to Palladio.

One day he stumbled over a description of the Temple of Vesta, a rotunda built by Numa Pompilius. Just the day before, he had measured the ruins of this round temple carefully, recognizing that the building was of importance but knowing nothing of its use. He found out that no man ever entered this temple. Instead, it housed virgins whose sole responsibility was to look after sacred objects.

Palladio was struck by the tale of what happened when some women such as Porphyria, Minutia, and Sextilia, all virgins, committed adultery. Their punishment was public humiliation and death. First, they were tied to a beam face down, their faces covered and the entire city placed in mourning. Then they were led to a sepulcher with one small hole and two windows. Within the frames of one window was placed a lighted lantern, and in the other, water, milk, and honey. The women passed these emblems of civility and were then shoved into the hole and buried alive.

Palladio shook his head in disbelief. He was glad he was not a woman. He exited the library that evening looking at the same sky that had seen such sad days, and pondered the ways of men.

When he and Daniele returned to the Barbaro palazzo in Venice, they agreed to collaborate on a villa at Maser, which Daniele, along with his younger brother Marcantonio, would inherit after the death of their elderly and ailing father. Palladio felt greatly relieved to have a new commission in the works.

Chapter Twenty-One

1557: VILLA BARBARO

Palladio was in Venice visiting the Barbaro palazzo once again. He was there to discuss the new Barbaro villa, for indeed, the patriarch of the family had finally died quietly in his bed. There was an existing building on the land at Maser, but both of the brothers were interested in designing a new villa that would combine the business of the farm with the pleasure of a summer home.

Marcantonio was sitting on the gold brocade couch, eating one of his sugared grapes and giving a lengthy criticism of a local politician. Marcantonio's genius was understanding the inner workings of the human heart and mind. He often spoke about who had been instrumental in getting some civic building made or who had managed to push through an important law. He saw the political system as a chess game: the balance of power between church and state, the personal proclivities of individuals, the lifetime struggles of those who could get him what he wanted. And what he wanted was to be in a position to make political change. He was hoping that soon he would hold the office of Savio di Terraferma, a position that would allow him to have some say in how Venice dealt with the property it held on the main land. Although Marcantonio was an amateur sculptor and architect, his heart was in the manipulation of men for the greater good.

As Palladio listened to the two brothers talk, he realized one of his major challenges would be to act as a design supervisor. The brothers had a plethora of design ideas, some that were excellent and some that would not stand the test of time and were destined to be out of fashion in a decade. He would act as an interlocutor, gently steering them away from the bad ideas. This project would require a most delicate dance, for both men were friends of his and it was essential that he not only keep them as friends, but also keep them friendly toward each other. Both brothers were politically and socially connected and had been instrumental in presenting Palladio as a competitive architect on several important projects.

When Marcantonio finally showed Palladio his sculptures, Palladio gracefully complimented him. Inside, however, his heart sank. Although the figures were technically perfect, Marcantonio had failed to bring them from material to life. The stone was still just stone. As Marcantonio led him around the studio, Palladio knew that Marcantonio's sculptures would have to be a major element in the design of the brothers' new house. Inwardly, Palladio sighed. This was the life of an architect, for it was client based; he rarely had complete control over the design.

As Palladio, Marcantonio, and Daniele talked in detail about the proposed villa, Palladio became enthralled with putting into practice some of the lessons he had learned while studying the baths in Rome. He was interested in creating a hydraulic system that would water all of the gardens and the *brolo* (orchards) and reach far down to the road below where troughs watered the tethered horses. He knew that Marcantonio would need a place to erect his statuary, so he conceived of a design that would feature a nymphaeum. Marcantonio could sculpt a series of beautiful young nymphs, spirits of nature, who would adorn the stone pond that could be built into the back hill where a year-round natural spring currently bubbled.

Palladio heard footsteps on the stairs outside of the piano nobile. Paolo Veronese, the great artist famous for his brilliantly colored paintings, entered the room. He pulled his green velvet cap off, scratched his short red hair, and smiled broadly. Marcantonio and Daniele offered him a place on the settee and a servant handed him a glass of wine. He was in fine fettle for he had just received an award, a gold chain for his participation on a team who had painted allegorical roundels on the ceiling of the Biblioteca Marciana. Palladio and the Barbaro brothers toasted his success.

The brothers were interested in commissioning Veronese to create the frescoes for their new home. Palladio was eager to meet this man, one of the most celebrated painters in Venice. Rumors abounded on how Veronese was able to coax such vibrant colors out of mere paint and many believed that he incorporated sapphires, rubies, pearls, and diamonds into the paint itself so that it would catch each ray of light. Furthermore, he was known not only for his ability to paint intricate allegorical works, but also for his biting wit.

Throughout the evening, he proved to be a clever companion with a barbed acerbic tongue that skewered the slovenly ways of certain members of the church as well as some of the greedier members of the doge's court. It was small wonder that his paintings famously featured dogs who seemed to laugh at the base nature of humans, and chubby putti who barely masked their glee at seeing the Ten Commandments disobeyed.

"We painters take the same liberties as poets and madmen," he said. Palladio and the Barbaro brothers appreciated that sentiment and the three men rose to their feet and toasted Veronese with yet another glass of wine. The evening finally came to an end when Veronese claimed fatigue and revealed that he needed to be back at Chiesa di San Sebastiano (Church of Saint Sebastian), where, as he put it, he had a liaison with a putti.

When the plans for the villa were finally completed, Palladio breathed a sigh of relief. The process, as he had intuited, had been mostly the work of a design diplomate. He often had found himself squarely between disagreeing brothers, and his major task had been to find a way through two seemingly irreconcilable designs.

Part of his strategy as an architect was to always focus on what he could learn from each project. Much of what he mastered during the design of the Villa Barbaro was how to beneficently manipulate the conversation and the focus so that a final decision could be reached. He was relieved when the villa design was finished and that it successfully incorporated the needs of the farm and of the family. The Barbaros had paid him well for his time, and for once, money was not the first thought of the day.

Chapter Twenty-Two

1557: VILLA EMO

Palladio always enjoyed the ride down the Grand Canal. It was an opportunity to move around effortlessly, relax, and see a constantly changing picture of a thriving Venice. Although it was still early in the day, the canal was already alive with barges carrying kegs of beer, bolts of silk, sacks of flour, and something new, maize. Palladio was on his way to see the Emo family to discuss a new villa.

1557 continued to be a great year. Two commissions would keep the family coffers at least half filled. Sometimes, Palladio wished he had chosen to be a merchant, for many of the people he met had made good money in trading silk, flour, and wheat.

A case in point was the Emo family, who had been instrumental in introducing this new world grain, maize, to the Italian diet. Immediately, people recognized it as a relatively inexpensive alternative to chickpeas, spelt, chestnut flour, and farro, and they prepared it in the same way by grinding it into a porridge or polenta. Palladio had heard that a good portion of the Emo lands had been sewn with maize.

The Palazzo Emo had been built directly on the canal, so when the gondolier swiftly steered his boat to the pier, Palladio only had to leap out of the gondola and take two steps before he was at the door. Servants led him into the main room on the second floor where Adrianna and her son, Leonardo the Younger, sat waiting. It was difficult to give the two people in the room the attention they deserved because the room commanded it all. It was not the most ornate room that Palladio had ever been in, or the richest, but there was something about its austere opulence that caught his eye and held it. It was like looking at a general who did not have to work hard to command.

The ceiling was coffered and made of a dark hardwood. Paintings crowned the tops of each of the doors and a rich red silk carpet was spread over the bright blue mosaic floor. After a few stolen glimpses, Palladio tore his eyes from the room and focused on the two people who had risen to greet him. Adrianna was tall with a pearled headdress and a soft green brocaded gown. Her neck was adorned with a complicated necklace of emeralds. All of this Palladio noticed in a moment, but it was her face that was the most decorative thing about her. She was one of those women who was lucky to have a face that telegraphed a lively spirit.

On that day, she was applying all of her abilities to ensure that a beautiful domicile would be ready for her son and his bride-to-be, Cornelia Grimani. Unlike many of the estates that Palladio had worked on, this piece of land had belonged to the

Emo family for centuries. It was a small part of a massive series of land purchases that had increased the family property and had been carried out by Giovanni Emo, Leonardo's grandfather, who was now long dead. Leonardo the Elder, Adrianna's husband, had died in 1540, leaving Adrianna to lead the family as best she could.

And her best was very good, Palladio was thinking as she laid out her plans. She was succinct.

"Our home needs to be a working farm with room for livestock, granaries, and dovecotes," she began, "but it also needs to be prestigious; a home that will present a vision of importance and power to anyone who visits. There must be no doubt that the person who leads this household knows what they are doing."

She looked at him directly. Palladio instinctively knew how difficult it must be for her to be the head of her household. He could only imagine the many ways, both large and small, that the men around her would try to erode her power. She had prepared a list of the requirements and she laid them in front of him with a flourish. Leonardo sat by, content to let his competent mother do all of the work. It allowed him to think about Cornelia's shining face.

After they had covered every possible requirement in detail, she smoothed down her green silk dress and leaned back, smiling. She placed her slim, cool fingers upon the page.

"And now, I place my trust in you. Design something brilliant."

And Palladio did. He was able to design a building without

interference from patrons who thought they knew better. He designed it the way he knew it should be designed.

One approached Leonardo and Cornelia's home via a long walkway that was perpendicular to the building itself. The walkway featured poplars that whispered in the slightest wind. The building had a grand exterior ramp that led to a classic porch with stately columns and a triangular pediment, and not only transported people from the ground level up to the first floor, but could also be used for drying crops. The pediment contained two winged Victories that held the Emo coat of arms in silver and red. The domicile was flanked on both sides by the *barchesse*, two long buildings with loggias that ran the length of the building and shielded the nobles as well as the commoners from the weather. Eleven arches on each side of the house defined the *barchesse's* main architectural impact simply and practically, giving the workers shelter as well as light to work by.

Although the *barchesse* was separated from the house by walkways that could be used to get to the rear of the property, the overall effect was that the three buildings were all one united front because Palladio had used the arches to unify the longitudinal facade. Two working dovecotes, which rose on each end, capped the *barchesse* so that squab could continue to be a staple for the table.

For the interior of the domicile, Palladio had perfected harmony in using rooms that related mathematically to each other. The ceilings were high; the interior entryways were elegant archways. The floors were a marble aggregate that allowed a myriad of colors to echo the colors of the frescoes which were painted by Battista Zelotti, who had worked with Veronese on the Biblioteca Marciana in Venice.

Palladio had been worried that his legacy would be filled with buildings that were tarnished or tempered by the wishes of his patrons. He envisioned a future in which students of architecture would review his life works and wonder at some of the choices that he had made, since all of the buildings were collaborations, and the patrons who had the money would ultimately be the determiners when there was a disagreement. And although Palladio had become a master at getting his own way while not appearing to do so, it was a great source of frustration for him. Like any artist who looked at his own work, he saw only the flaws.

His greatest wish had been that he could design a beautiful building that would express his ideas completely. A building that reflected all of his aesthetics, all of his thoughts about Roman classicism, all of his ideas about how to combine the practical with the beautiful. The Villa Emo was that building. As he continued to work on his book, he was able to transfer the designs of the Villa Emo verbatim.

Chapter Twenty-Three

1560: SAN GIORGIO

Allegradonna had not been happy when Palladio finally announced that he would need to live in Venice for a while. At first, he had suggested that he go alone, leave her behind. But that idea had not gone over well.

He sat her down at the kitchen table and they discussed it like adults. That is, Allegradonna threw her ink pot at him. Palladio, with his vestment stained in apple ink, raised his eyebrows. This was not usual for Allegradonna, and that very fact made him pay special attention.

Allegradonna burst into tears. Palladio managed to understand her though her hands were in front of her face.

"I am always alone," she sobbed. "I am reduced to this kitchen, this garden, this house, while you are gone at your dinners, your trips, your visits to every palazzo, every villa. You must have women in these places, for why would you want to be gone so much of the time?"

Palladio took her hands in his, revealing Allegradonna's face, which was blotchy and tear-stained.

"I see no other woman but you, my dear," he said, stroking her temple with his index finger. "For you are my light, my love, the mother of my children. You are still the smartest, funniest, and most beautiful woman at any table, in any house, in any city in God's creation."

She looked at him with her liquid brown eyes.

He smiled. "Besides, don't the children keep you busy?"

Allegradonna tilted her head and looked at him as though he were an idiot.

"They are not children anymore. They are adults and they are finding their own way in the world. There is not much I can do when they dance in late at night. You see, I am their mother, and at their age, a mother is like the family dog—a thing to pay attention to only when one wants to."

Palladio led her to her chair in front of the fire and put a few more logs on. This would require some thinking.

By the end of the night, they had arrived at a plan. For a brief while, they would keep two houses, one in Venice and the other in Vicenza. And they would shuttle back and forth as Palladio's work required. They would take everyone with them—their children, the servants, even the dogs would come. Allegradonna, using her accounting gifts, had figured out how they could pay for it, although money would be in short supply. And Palladio could start to extend his reach to Venice, for that was where the work was.

The first thing that Palladio noticed about the abbot of the Benedictine Congregazione di Santa Giustina was his rings, and he was sure that was by design. Clad all in black—which gave the community the moniker of the Black Monks—the only color on the abbot was on his hands, where gold rings sparkled with red, green, and blue. In all other ways, the man was the picture of a solemn and austere lifestyle. Palladio sat in front of the abbot's large walnut desk in his office near the refectory that he hoped he would be able to redesign.

The abbot spoke. The large hall where the monks ate was in severe decline. The roof leaked and swallows had managed to find their way in so that the three-story roof had become an aviary. When one of the swallows had—and here the abbot managed a rare smile—managed to excrete into his soup, it was clear that enough was enough.

The abbot rose and they headed toward the refectory. As they walked through the cool halls, priests and deacons popped in and out of doors, carrying buckets, flowers, and hymnals. The abbot blessed them all with a wave of his hand when they scurried by. As they entered the refectory, he described the job that he wanted Palladio to do. They were suddenly alone in the massive hall and his words echoed from the walls.

The refectory would be designed in collaboration with Paolo Veronese, for he had been commissioned to make a large-scale painting based on the day that Christ turned water into wine. The abbot envisioned a painting that was massive—a length of four carriages end to end and almost as high. The colors would be brilliant. The abbot had specified that lapis lazuli, a precious metal, be used to create the blues, and he wanted Veronese to include as many figures as possible. The painting would be monumental in size, population, and impact.

Palladio was fine with this stipulation for he had worked with Veronese when designing and building the Barbaro villa. Unlike some other painters, Veronese had proven to be a willing collaborator, and together he and Palladio had designed an environment that was pleasing both from the architect's point of view and the painter's. In the Hall of Olympus, Marcantonio had wanted the paintings to reflect his household: his wife, Giustiniana; the wet-nurse; her youngest son; and the family pets, a parrot and a spaniel.

He and Veronese had enjoyed a good laugh about that spaniel. Named Scampo ("Scamp"), this dog ran the entire household to such a degree that Veronese and Palladio agreed it should have its own little room with its own painting, which was called ever after "The Room of the Little Dog." Marcantonio was delighted, for he, too, had a sense of humor and knew that Scampo was the true head of the household.

The abbot and Palladio spent most of the afternoon talking about the needed qualities of the dining room. The abbot wanted two large washstands so the monks could wash themselves before eating. Perhaps red, he thought, and Palladio immediately envisioned them on a floor with a red and white design. Two thermal windows and a barrel-vaulted ceiling would be grand enough for both men and God, said the abbot. Palladio agreed, thinking about how the light would splash through the windows in the morning and light the ceiling so the lines of the vault would be revealed as architectural sculpture.

Before the two men had parted, Palladio had a clear idea of what the abbot wanted, and perhaps more importantly, what was needed. He promised he would have designs for the abbot within six weeks. When he departed, the abbot blessed him, solemnly waving his hands in the air, his rings once again on display.

This refectory job soon led to a more substantial opportunity. Palladio was asked to design the church. The abbot's rings had been a clue that this project would spare no expense and could afford to be built primarily from expensive white marble. It would be dedicated to two venerated Christian martyrs, Saint Stephen and Saint George. Saint Stephen was known as the first Christian martyr, for he had been stoned to death by an angry mob, and Saint George—depending on who you were talking to—had died either by beheading or by a slow torture that occurred over a period of seven years.

The refectory should be filled with story, the abbot said. It should be a place where people can see the stories written out in carved relief. The stories and the space needed to remind people of their duty to God and the role that they can play in continuing a religious life.

Palladio envisioned an impressive portico that could be seen from the mainland. A double tympanum with four colossal columns. Statuary of angels and the saints would cap each angle of the roof and people would need to look up, to force their vision heavenward, in order to take in the enormity of the will of God. The doorway of walnut would be equally tall, echoing the theme of the immenseness of the heavens and the smallness of man. The white of the marble would be seen in the reflections of the Canale di San Marco. Small boats would pass by and the reflections of this great church would ripple and break apart as though also a reflection of the short time we spend on this earth. For eventually, Palladio knew, we all ripple and break, dissipate and disappear.

The inside would feature a line of columns on either side that led the eye naturally to the highly decorated altar in front of them. The church would include a dome and a series of arches that would soar over the heads of the worshipers.

Palladio excitedly drew a few sketches as he talked with the abbot. He quickly sketched the arches. His drawing skills were one of his finest assets for they could immediately convey a feeling of what it would be like to stand in the space.

The abbot, with his thin austere face and his flashing rings, was a man of opinion. He immediately began asking questions. He laid wizened fingers upon his chin, looking at the sketches with a squint. "How tall are these doors? What will it feel like when you enter? How much will the building cost if we make it out of marble?" After each question he would pause, waiting for an immediate answer.

Palladio would not be cornered into answering these critical questions so swiftly. He parlayed the answers.

"The doors will be as tall as trees. When people enter, they will feel the smallness of humanity and the greatness of God. I will need to make many calculations before I can give you exact numbers."

The abbot looked at him from under his bushy eyebrows and paused, not speaking. Palladio wondered at that moment if he had lost the job. But the abbot simply asked that Palladio build a model for him. Palladio was more than happy to do so, for this project would be a masterwork. And a masterwork was not only a lifetime opportunity to create a major edifice—it also meant more money.

Chapter Twenty-Four

1561: A YEAR OF UPS AND DOWNS

Palladio and his family were back in Vicenza. Although Palladio loved Venice, he was most comfortable in his rented house, with its small square of garden in the back, its hearth, and his desk, which was positioned over the window so he could look down on the street.

It was a special day, so he would dress in his finest, which included his best linen shirt, his silk striped netherstocks, a leather jerkin (the one without stains), and his red brocaded jacket, for the weather had once again turned nippy. He finished dressing before sunrise and joined Allegradonna in the kitchen, where she was already baking bread. She gave him a hug and presented a hot tray of *cannellini ricci*, a twisted bread of cinnamon and sugar. She had taken it directly out of the oven and it was still steaming. The smell of cinnamon entered his nose. The smell of home.

Allegradonna took off her floury apron and spun in front of

him. She, too, was dressed up, radiant in her red-rose silk dress and skirt. The lightweight dress shimmered and fluttered in the air as she spun around, while the bodice kept her decent.

They walked arm in arm to the town square where it seemed that the entire population of Vicenza had turned out for the christening of the Basilica, on which the northern and western arches were finally completed. As Palladio stood with his wife on the platform that had been especially built for the occasion, his eyes watered. It had taken twelve years of painstaking labor to finish this part of the building. Sometimes, Palladio had wondered if he would live to see his Basilica completed. Many of the structures he had set in motion had been stalled and were left half finished. He tried not to view each unfinished building like an unfinished piece of music, but truly, that is exactly how it felt to him.

This day, however, he stood before a master work, for he knew that he had saved it, improved it, and changed the square forever.

Vicenza's finest were on the platform with him—men and women who had helped him with money and political clout. He wished that Trissino could see this day, that he could be sitting next to him with Allegradonna. Trissino would have made a speech and been honored as he should have been honored, for it was he who had taken a firm hand and wrestled this troubled building into a new existence.

Giovanni flitted into his mind as well. So many good people had contributed to this project. So many who had already passed on and were sitting with God.

As it turned out, there were plenty of living people who made many long speeches. Men who stole credit and some who pushed it away. Palladio was neither of these. When it came time for him to address the crowd, he focused on Trissino and Giovanni, and the other men who were responsible for getting movement on the building. He complimented them for pushing the project through the entropic influences of time and money—the lack thereof—and praised them for their visionary abilities. He asked that the people truly look at the building and see it for what it was: a record of history, a recognition of the magistrates who ruled Vicenza with a judicious hand, and a handsome place of commerce, for the bottom floor housed a jewelry shop, a dress store, a millinery, and a cobbler, all of whom were represented on the platform as well.

He asked that they envision the second-story reconstruction, which would begin as soon as there was money in the public coffers to support the endeavor. He reminded people that the job was not done, but would need constant and diligent supporters to bolster the continued construction of the building as surely as a flying buttress.

The crowd cheered for they genuinely liked Palladio. He was that rare man who could dine with both commoner and nobleman alike.

Silla, his youngest son, sidled into Palladio's studio and fingered the tapestry on the northern wall. He was the steadiest of Palladio's sons and had grown into a thoughtful young man who could be counted on for almost any task. Silla was the son who had expressed the most interest in the family business and Palladio had responded by taking him along on many of his trips to Venice and once to Trieste. Silla studiously paid attention as though he knew that there would be a time when he would be the one who needed to understand the intricacies of the architectural process.

He was easy to educate, bright as the sun when it came to understanding the complexities of mathematics and accounting. He usually did what his father told him to do. His one vice was food, which he ate a little too much of, and in this way he was his mother's bane, for she could never truly fill him up.

Silla was loyal and brave, which he proved one night when he saved his sister from drowning in the Bacchiglione River. Without a hint of a momentary hesitation he had kicked off his sandals and plunged in without thinking. Fortunately, the river was only four feet deep and it turned out that all Zenobia had needed to do was stand up.

Now, Silla seemed fascinated by every book spine, for he peered at each one as if one of them were going to tell him the meaning of life. Palladio watched him with curiosity, wondering how long it would take him to say what he needed to say. Silla seemed uncomfortable in his clothes, like he needed to scratch his way out of them.

Palladio let him stew a while longer before he finally said, "Sit down before you fall down."

Silla sat down quickly like a felled tree and then poured out his troubles.

Palladio had thought that he had been keeping Silla busy. Too busy to get into any real trouble. But trouble, like water, finds its own way. Neither Allegradonna or Palladio knew that Silla had been having a passionate affair with one of the house servants, Donna Isabetta. Donna was well liked. She went about her world with a will, never had a bad word for anyone, and would sing when she was hanging out the wash. She could read and she even wrote a little poetry which, it turned out, she had started showing to Silla. Love poetry. And from the very first line, when she likened him to a swan, he was hooked.

Silla had come to consult with his father, There was a problem. An age-old problem. Donna was going to have a child. But for Palladio, the solution was simple: Marry her.

Silla was stunned. He couldn't marry a servant, he said, a maid who washed his clothes.

Palladio felt as though one of his own columns had fallen over and crushed him. He roared, "Your mother was a servant! And she has washed your clothes and brought food to the table, and mended your socks and cleaned your shoes and combed that gnarly head of yours, and somehow, she forgot to clean out the space between your ears or mend the place in your hollow chest!"

Now Silla was truly shocked. He had never heard his father lose his temper before and he was known as a man who never raised his voice.

When Allegradonna found out, her ire was much worse than Palladio's, for she went to church weekly and believed that having a child before wedlock was truly a mortal sin. Unlike many women, however, she did not solely blame the girl but blamed the boy in these manners with equal wrath.

She started off slowly. "What do you mean she is with child? Whose child is she with?"

Silla rubbed his hands together. This was not going to be easy.

Allegradonna crossed her arms. "I suppose she is like the Virgin Mary and she will have perhaps the daughter of God."

Silla laughed weakly.

"Silla," Allegradonna continued, "I thought we raised you so that you were smart. So that you were kind." She was winding up. "So that you have a brain in your head! How could you do something so stupid, so sinful, so wrong? How could you shame our family like this? How could you bring this into our home? Donna is a good girl. I don't blame her. I blame you. Someone who should know better. Someone who is an ethical, caring person! Someone I thought I knew!"

Silla looked at the floor.

Within a week Silla was married to Donna.

Palladio found himself pacing nervously behind the stucco theatrical flats. He knew every inch of them, since he had designed and built them himself. He wiped the sweat from his brow—it was as though he were possessed by the ghost of Trissino, for he could not sit and watch the first performance of Trissino's *Sofonisba*, but instead needed to be watching from the side. Even up close, the walls looked as though they were made of true

Carthaginian stone, as they were lit with small glass bulbs filled with oil that had been placed in strategic niches. They looked like what they were meant to portray: a palazzo in Carthage during the Second Punic War.

Palladio found his heart stirring as he watched the tragic title character, Sofonisba, a doomed noblewoman trapped between heaving political, economic, and military circumstances, drain the hemlock from her jeweled goblet. As she fell to the ground, he found a tear coursing down his cheek. *Trissino should be here*, he thought. An artist should see their own work.

The Greek chorus solemnly commented about this tragedy, not only the one on stage but also the one in Palladio's heart. This was the chorus that Trissino had included only during one of the last rewrites, and Palladio had murmured under his breath, "See Trissino? It works fine." Trissino had also used free verse—a risky choice—but the actors were wearing the language like a new coat.

As the play ended and the audience applauded, Palladio reflected on the eternity of art. He knew Trissino's play would live on. Palladio spied several influential playwrights in the crowd, people who would take note of Trissino's main innovation—his use of this new style of language, never heard in Italy. They would steal that innovation and make it their own, for that was the way with art. Imitation was surely the way to go down in history. Yes, if nothing else, Trissino would be known for this.

Chapter Twenty-Five

1564: CELEBRATIONS AND MORE WORK

It was right that Palladio had only one daughter, for the rarity of an excellent essence only made it more valuable. Zenobia, named after the third-century queen of Palmyra, was the kind of girl who spread only joy. When she was younger, and Palladio was home, she would insist on sitting in his lap, settling in it like a content lamb. As she grew up, she still wanted to sit in the throne of his lap even when she could no longer fit comfortably and needed to drape herself over him like a long-legged calf.

Unlike her mother, she was not a serious thinker, but rather a wry observer, pointing out the foibles of men and women as though she were plucking fruit. When she was in the market with Palladio, he would attempt to point out the perfectly carved volutes, the spiral scroll structures of a classic Ionic capital, but she preferred to see the one sagging sock on the man who limped before her. She laughed her way to adulthood. Sometimes

Palladio was worried that no man would ever see her merits, for he had observed that she sometimes even laughed while at Mass.

One day, while in somewhat of a sour mood, he had commented that being with her was like being with a dog, since he had always believed the reason people appreciated dogs is that they made them laugh. She stared at him with her large dark eyes, and for a moment, he thought he might have finally offended her. She suddenly bent over at the waist and he feared she was crying. But when she stood back up again, he saw that she was red in the face from trying not to laugh. She finally exploded with a bray that could have been heard in the next town. From that moment on, when they were alone and she wanted to pester him slightly, she would bark a little as though she were a small and annoying dog.

When he would come home and was worn from the challenges of trying to get the landowner, his architects, the stone masons, and the city officials all marching in the same general direction, she would charm him with some light story, an observation of human frailty that would make him remember that this work, his work, was a small effort in the eyes of God. She managed to give him perspective, which was sometimes all he needed to begin the process all over again the next day.

He was quite unprepared when a man by the name of Battista della Fede came to visit. He was shown in and immediately got down on one knee. Palladio had the fortune of seeing his scalp up close. He tried to get Battista to stand up so that he could get a better look at him, but it took Palladio several attempts before the man finally stood. He was short. Shorter than the average man, and for a moment Palladio entertained the idea that perhaps that was why it took him so long to stand.

In addition to being short, he looked rather like an owl with overextended eyes and bushy eyebrows that dominated his face. The moment he opened his mouth, however, Palladio took an immediate liking to the fellow, for his voice was as resonant as the stringed lira da braccio. He had a way about him, a kind of sincerity, that Palladio felt drawn to. As Battista explained, he was a goldsmith—a goldsmith who wanted to marry Palladio's daughter, Zenobia.

It was June, the month when everyone wanted to get married, and Zenobia was no different. The Roman goddess Junio watched over all the marriages in June and would make sure that all areas of domesticity went well.

Zenobia stopped outside of the dome that her father had recently completed. She sat down on the stone step and, with a needle and thread, finished the last inch of her hemline. Now her wedding dress was complete. Having finished up yet one more task on a long list of rituals, she entered the Vicenza Cathedral, eager to get her marriage day started.

Palladio sat in the front row and watched as the priest married off his only daughter. He was content. He knew Battista to be a gentle man, a skilled craftsman, and someone who was wise with his money. Even more importantly, it was clear he adored Zenobia and Zenobia adored him. As they stared at each other past the droning priest, Palladio could see the mutual love in their eyes. He felt a certain magnetism between the two and it seemed that only the priest's presence prevented them from rushing to crush each other in a loving embrace.

He glanced at Allegradonna. She caught his eye and smiled. For a moment, she was the young raven-haired girl who would not look away. He took her hand and held it until the ceremony was over. He had married well and he trusted that Zenobia had married well, too. Although he was losing Zenobia—his little honey bee, as he used to call her—he sensed that she would soon deliver new honey bees that he could dandle on his knee. Perhaps being a grandfather was something he would relish.

He stared up at the dome that he had designed. Such a wonderful invention where stresses were equally applied. He wished that the stresses of life could be so easily spread out so one could have space to take them in and deal with them one at a time. He sent a prayer to God that the dome above his only daughter would continue to shelter her throughout life. For there was his beautiful child standing under it, kissing her new husband. For the moment, this one moment, all was well.

It was Allegradonna's birthday. Palladio had made sure that he would be home, for he had a very special gift for her. It was a light and breezy September day. Most of it would be like any other day until evening, when a special dinner had been arranged. It would be a family affair with Leonida, Marcantonio, Silla, Zenobia, and her new husband, Battista, all in attendance.

The afternoon sun was just starting to make its way down to the horizon when they heard voices.

Allegradonna greeted Zenobia and Battista at the door with kisses on both sides of their cheeks. They had come laden with gifts of sweetmeats and flowers. Marcantonio was next, carrying a bottle of chianti and a wedge of fontina. Silla and his bride, Donna Isabetta, were close behind. Donna Isabetta carried their child, a boy whom they had named Pietro after Palladio's father. He was plump and cheery and proudly carried his first new toy, a rattle in the shape of a pig. They waited for Leonida to arrive, and at last he came, bumping his shoulder against the side jambs of the door as he entered, weaving his way toward the table. Palladio put his arm around Allegradonna's shoulder for he knew how worried she was about this son, their only child who did not seem to be thriving.

Leonida plunked himself down in a chair and beamed, loudly wishing his mother a happy birthday. The rest of Allegradonna's children swiftly took over the room, talking, laughing, and ignoring the brother with the face that was shining from too much drink.

All in all, the dinner was a success. Allegradonna received a small gold chain from Zenobia and Battista; a new cooking spoon from Marcantonio; packets of tomato, cucumber, and pepper seeds from Silla and Donna Isabetta; and a sloppy kiss from Leonida, who had forgotten the tradition of bringing birthday gifts. Palladio waited to be last. He had wrapped his gift in treasured paper which alone signified its worth. Allegradonna was sitting at the table, and as he handed it to her, she looked at him with her dark eyes. She could tell this was special.

She untied the brown twine and began unwrapping the paper carefully. It was a book. A rare thing. She gasped with pleasure when she saw what it was. *De Honesta Voluptate et Valetudine* (*On Honest Indulgence and Good Health*). A cookbook. It contained not only a collection of recipes that would soothe the ills of the day, but also advice on sleep, the benefits of fresh air, and how to properly set a table. The 1508 Venetian edition. She jumped up and hugged Palladio. Palladio laughed, kissing her. He knew that she would treasure the gift for the rest of her life.

Later that night, after Allegradonna had gone to bed, he thumbed through it. It was a book that was designed to be useful to everyday life. Its advice was solid and addressed all aspects of life. He stared at the ceiling, thinking.

What if his book on architecture could be as useful? He sighed, realizing it had been weeks since he had been able to get back to it. What might a practical book look like? Certainly, the ingredients would be critical. Instead of flour, eggs, and water, he would talk about sand, stone, and bricks. He thought about what would be most helpful. Specifics. He would specify the differences between sea sand, pit sand, and river sand. He would explain to architects that pit sand was best, with its variety of colors—black, red, white, and ash—and tell them about pozzolana, a sand that when mixed with water immediately turned to a kind of cement. And he would talk about the bad kinds of sand. The sand that, when laid upon a white cloth, would stain. For that was the kind of sand that was impure and could later result in the sprouting of fig trees and fir, something that could destroy a building in a few years.

He went to his desk and began to make notes. This would be the book of his life. The book that would, with luck, give him some measure of immortality.

The moment that thought struck him, he felt chagrined. Immortality. No man should wish for such a thing, for God had made immortality a reward that only he could give.

He closed the book on his notes and looked over at the sleeping form of his wife. The book could wait.

Palladio tramped down the Contrà Santi Apostoli, a street that led to the ancient Teatro Berga. He was armed with all of his surveying tools, which he kept in a large, sturdy bag that he could carry on his back. The Berga theater fascinated him, as it was a Roman ruin in his own hometown. He had been thinking about starting the arduous task of measuring it, but he never had found the time until now.

Little was known about it. The theater was rumored to have been built by the Giulio-Claudia family, the first Roman imperial dynasty. The family included five emperors—Augustus, Tiberius, Caligula, Claudius, and Nero. He wondered which one was directly responsible for building such a beautiful theater so far from Rome. Many people knew that it was briefly owned by

Holy Roman Emperor Otto III and that it had landed in a long-dead bishop's coffers. It was he who had allowed it to become a prison. And now it was in ruins. Palladio clicked his tongue to think that such a once-beautiful structure had been allowed to be overrun with prisoners and the guards who kept them.

He clambered into the ruins, noticing multicolored marbles amid the dirt and clay. He came upon a stone arm, a woman's arm with graceful fingers holding a palm frond. He imagined this formerly lovely statue among these men who perhaps could not appreciate these things. He sighed. Buildings exhibited the foibles of man. But then he had a second thought. Perhaps these prisoners, with art and music withheld from them, would appreciate these sculptures even more than those who were surrounded by art. The thought made him shake his head, wondering at the workings of his own mind.

He recognized the white limestone from the Costozza quarries, which for centuries had been the stone of choice for the Romans. He saw the curving line of the broken *scaenae frons*, the back wall of the theater, which would have been filled with statues and tall Corinthian columns.

He set to work. The southern part, which had been the actual theater, had a diameter of about eighty-two meters. Palladio stood and stretched his back. At that size, thousands of people could have seen the theatrical production. He imagined the collective roars when Oedipus defeated the monstrous sphinx, the sobs when Medea killed her sons, the applause at the end of each performance.

By the end of the week he had taken all the measurements he could. The northern portico, depending on how he read the ruins, was between seventy and eighty meters. This meant that the theater could hold more than 5,000 spectators. He climbed to the center of what he thought was the stage. Although the theater was in ruins, he could still see the outlines, imagine the building as it was. He made a few quick sketches while they were still in his mind. He drew the back wall two stories tall, filled with niches that contained statuary and columns that soared well above the actors' heads. Indeed, the theater would dwarf the actors, emphasizing the theme that humans are only puppets controlled by the gods.

Trissino had been an ardent appreciator of theater and had made sure to expose Palladio to as many theater productions as possible. When in Rome, they had seen several productions and Trissino had made him read the plays of Seneca. Palladio plied Trissino with questions about stage design, costumes, and even the fine art of wigs.

For Trissino, the theater was a direct reflection of culture and ideological change. It spoke what could not be spoken. It presented the flame of ideas that could be seen through the filter of humor or pathos. A play provided the necessary distance to allow people to hear an original or outrageous idea. It infiltrated the mind and allowed the new thought to take harbor there like a small cat. In that way, it was rebellious and insubordinate, mutinous and incendiary. If Trissino could have been anything, he would have wanted to be a successful playwright.

As Palladio surveyed the ruin in front of him, he brushed away a tear. He missed his dear friend and benefactor. The world seemed darker and colder since his death.

Chapter Twenty-Six

1569: LEONIDA KILLS AND ORAZIO GETS A LAW DEGREE

Palladio had been sitting by the fire in his favorite chair. He had built it to his own specifications. Leather back and seat, carved wooden arms and legs with wooden knobs on each corner. The knobs had been carved as though they were solid balls of vines. He could reach up, grab them, and stretch his back. Such an invention.

The house was quiet, the kind of cottony quiet that is formed around sleeping people. The only lit candle was on the table beside him. He had been attempting to read, but the light was too dim. Perhaps he should investigate those odd things that the monks put over their eyes and used while poring over their ornate books. They said it helped their eyesight.

He was just about to retire to bed when he heard banging on the door. It was faint, heard through many substantial walls, but he could tell someone was desperate, someone who knew him needed to get in. He waited. He heard the wooden door creak open (he should oil those hinges) and muffled voices. Moments later, Leonida burst into the room. He was haggard and wild-eyed, with a terrible pinch to his mouth, his hands gripping and loosening convulsively. When he saw his father, he burst into long shuddering sobs.

Palladio sat him down and made him drink a glass of wine. Leonida drank it down in two gulps. He yanked his black overcoat off, revealing a white shirt splashed with red. Blood. Palladio involuntarily gasped.

Leonida, suddenly quiet, whispered two words: "Alessandro Camera."

Palladio could not help saying at that moment, "Thank God. Someone else's blood."

Leonida suddenly plunged his head into his hands and began running his fingers through his hair. "Father. I killed him."

When Palladio heard these words, he felt a complicated rush of emotions: horror, shock, and then anger, for Leonida had always been the problematic son. Silla was undeniably loyal and skilled enough to follow in his father's footsteps; Orazio was studious and thoughtful; and Marcantonio was well on his way to being a skilled stone mason. But Leonida had been a wild child from birth, bent on breaking the rules just to see if he could. At every turn, he had pushed against some invisible wall of decorum and expectations. His attitude was that of a spoiled child who knew that he flew under the protection of his father, who in turn flew under the protection of Trissino.

And so he did not work. He was not interested in study or the pursuit of knowledge which was everything to his father.

Instead, as he insisted, "he knew how to enjoy life rather than blowing dust off the ancient pages in order to decipher them." He enjoyed wine far too much and the women of other men were especially appealing to him. Thus, Alessandro Camera.

As Leonida tried to explain to Palladio that night, Alessandro Camera's wife was too beautiful for one man to contain. Instead, she spilled out and over this one man like a perfect wine. Truly, it had been her fault, for she had stared at him repeatedly over the duck, the stag, and the boar.

And he was helpless when she cornered him one late night in a remote hallway at the back of Alessandro's house and led him to her own bedroom. According to her, she was married to a tyrant, a beast, someone who did nothing for her heart, nothing for her soul, and certainly nothing for the rest of her. In Leonida's telling, he was the hero of this story. He had brought his knife to the dinner that night because she had sent a servant warning him. Alessandro knew all and was out for his blood. It was in self-defense, Leonida said, as he picked at the blood that was drying on his shirt.

Palladio was many things, but he was not a violent man. Yes, as a very young man, he had felt the gorge rise in his heart against his first master, who he knew had been instrumental in the death of his first real friend, but time had dulled his penchant for violence and now he could not understand this human tendency. It was as foreign to him as a faraway language. But others, like his own son, embraced violence like a lover.

Violence was a way of life for many of the noblemen. Some, used to a life on the battlefield, came home and were bored by peace. These men stirred up trouble with relish, picking fights in taverns, at dinner parties, and on the street. They felt that they needed to keep in practice and sparring left them cold and removed. They yearned for the heat of battle and since battles were, for the moment, not an active phenomenon, they orchestrated duels, manipulating the young men who were short on brains and quick with white hot tempers. Many times, usually during the heat of high summer, Palladio had seen funeral processions, with their sobbing black-draped women and their stunned children, trudging down the streets toward the Maggiore Cemetery.

And now, here was his own son, drenched in the blood of another man.

Leonida flew into a panic and stood up. "I'm going to run, Father," he said in an uncharacteristically small voice. "I'll hide myself in the Dolomites. Perhaps I'll go to France."

As he rushed for the door, Palladio stood in his way. He pushed his son back into the chair and plied him with another glass of wine.

"You will not run," he said, matching Leonida's hushed voice. "You will not run. You will face what you have done. The law will be the law and if God is with us, you will be absolved of this sordid tragedy."

Leonida, his head in his hands, agreed.

The day that Leonida stood trial had all the makings of a perfect day. It was sunny without being hot, cloudy without being cool.

Birds sang as though they would never die and a comforting breeze lifted the spirits of all who felt it. But the Palladio family felt none of these things. Instead, they were sealed in a stifling room with too many people and too little air.

The magistrate Tommaso Morosini sat at his elevated desk, his white bushy hair sticking out at right angles from his round head. Palladio, Allegradonna, Zenobia, Silla, and Orazio took up the front row. Marcantonio had taken a job in Venice to work in the sculptor Alessandro Vittoria's workshop, so he was absent, but he had sent a message of support that Palladio knew now resided in Leonida's right breast pocket.

Leonida, who had always had the air of a dashing bon vivant, now sat in the defendant's chair looking shrunken, his chest caved inward, his shoulders curved forward.

It looked bad for Leonida. He had brought a knife to the house that night, which indicated he knew that there would be trouble and was prepared. The word "premeditated" echoed repeatedly off of the claustrophobic walls in the windowless room. The lovely Signora Camera sat four rows back, obscured by layers of black silk tulle; only her slender white hands, constantly pushing at her cuticles, betrayed her state of mind. The rest of the Camera family were a jumble of intense emotions: rage, sorrow, belligerence. They continually popped up and shouted in anger and Morosini had his hands full keeping order in his courtroom.

There was a long train of witnesses, since the dinner had been for a party of twenty. One by one, they testified to the brutality of the murder. Leonida had struck Camera in the face.

Blood had spurted everywhere. Women had rushed from the room and one slender man had vomited into the fireplace. A doctor had been called who could do nothing for the victim, as the knife had plunged directly into his heart, killing him almost instantly. Signora Camera had sat quietly at the table with her mouth slightly open, holding a glass of red wine but never drinking from it. Her face and her hair had been spattered with her husband's blood and several of the witnesses remarked how she had raised her hand and unknowingly smeared it obscenely across her face.

The knife had proven exceptionally interesting to the prosecutor, as it was made of Damascus steel. Even in his distraught mind, Palladio wondered where Leonida had obtained such an expensive weapon. Knives made of Damascus steel were known to be flexible, tough, and able to cut a human hair. The prosecutor must have loved knives, for he took precious time describing the blade with its curious watery pattern and the fact that no one really knew how it was made. All Palladio knew was that it had killed a man.

The evidence was overwhelmingly against Leonida. The magistrate went out of the room to deliberate. Palladio felt his heart dying in his chest. His own son would die on the gallows, his feet twitching, his covered face twisting grotesquely from side to side. Leonida, headstrong and impervious to childhood whippings, had grown up to this moment. Palladio groped for Allegradonna's hand. When he found it, he grasped it like a drowning man grasps a log. The two waited for the verdict.

Morosini entered the room after only a half hour. He

seemed in a good mood and there was a spring in his step that wasn't there before. Zenobia rose, stood behind her mother, and put reassuring hands on her shoulders. Allegradonna reached up and placed her hands on Zenobia's. The family was ready to hear the worst.

But Morosini surprised everyone. He ruled that Leonida had acted in self-defense. As the words came from Morosini's mouth, Leonida looked as though he were waking from a dream. He shook himself. He straightened his shoulders, ran a sure hand through his hair, and grinned, displaying beautiful white teeth.

Palladio saw several of his friends, Porto, the Thiene brothers, and Daniele Barbaro return to the room, and guessed the scene that had played out in the magistrate's private chambers. They had saved his son. His benefactors had not only rescued him from obscurity and poverty—they now saved him from heartbreak and ignominy. Leonida would live and the family would be spared the black mark of murder.

Leonida joined his family as they filed out of the court-room. He had already regained his rooster strut. Palladio's heart cracked, but did not break. He had a son. Just not the son he would have desired.

Several months after the trial, Paolo Veronese paid him a visit. The moment he stepped into the room, Palladio knew that something was wrong. His face was uncharacteristically stormy and his body was as stiff as a tree.

"I've come to talk to you about the trial," he said, and Palladio sat him down in the chair in front of the fire. Veronese was silent, repressing words so plentiful they choked him.

"Go on, Paolo. Say what you must say," returned Palladio, sitting in the chair next to him.

"You as well as I know that Leonida's trial was a sham. He was under the protection of your patrons." He bolted out of his chair. "How can you live with yourself? How can you look your son in the eye and know that he is guilty of murder?"

Palladio blanched as though Veronese had hit him. He seemed to shrink two inches.

"Paolo, you must leave now," he said quietly as he rose from his chair. "You do not know what it is like to have a son like Leonida."

"And for that I am grateful," Veronese spit out and, grabbing his hat, fled out the door.

Palladio collapsed back into the chair. It was true—he relied on these men, all of these men, for everything. His career was built on friendships, on easy camaraderie, for a man of his class could not hope to move forward in the circles he required without those friendships. In his heart, he knew that Veronese was right. Although he had not directly paid the magistrate off, one of his many wealthy friends surely had.

Palladio threw a teacup into the fire, where it shattered and remained until the next day when Allegradonna swept it up.

Life can be seen as a series of highs and lows. Although the saga of Leonida's murder trial was a low, it was soon followed by a high. In November, Orazio received his law degree. The entire family traveled to Padua to see Orazio, somber in his brilliant burgundy robe and matching stole, receive his parchment diploma proclaiming that he could now practice law. The family celebrated by having dinner at a popular *osteria*, Nane della Giulia. Giulia, a laughter-filled woman with a body as round as a ball, served them herself while regaling them with stories of splashing orzo and escaped chickens. By the time they left, they were stuffed with warm food and worn out from laughter. That night, they left Orazio at his home, and even Leonida gave his serious brother a hug before departing.

One night after Palladio had returned from Padua, he found himself in a rare moment of relaxation. He was in the small back courtyard, bundled up against the December cold, thinking about Christmas and the locket he had already bought as a gift for Allegradonna. His thoughts turned to his sons, each one so different they might have personally shaped the clay they were born from.

Leonida was his firstborn. Palladio had heard him from the next room squalling like a cat. He had arrived kicking and screaming and never stopped. He was a child who was never satisfied with his food, never eager to work hard, and interested only in escaping the house to play *trottola* with his friends.

When Palladio had played *trotolla* as a child, they had called it "turbo." Palladio himself had taught it to his eldest son. He showed Leonida how to draw a circle in the dirt and scratch out ten numbered sections. He taught him how to wind a wooden top with string and then pull the string, forcing the top to spin in one or more of the sections, willing the top to stray into the higher numbered sections. Palladio had enjoyed the game, but he knew when to play and when to work. Leonida never seemed to understand work was a necessary part of life; he would rather play any game and make any wager. Girls caught his eye early.

Palladio sighed. Perhaps he had not been strict enough, present enough. Were all children the direct result of omissions and parental failures or were they somehow already themselves by the time they were born? He thought about his other children.

Marcantonio was unlike Leonida in almost all ways. He was a born worker, a studious thinker, and a competent designer. He had followed in his father's footsteps, working at Giacomo da Porlezza and Girolamo Pittoni's workshop as a stonecutter while still a young man. He was brilliant with a chisel, coaxing fine shaped leaves, putti, and cow-skull bucrania that were so eerily realistic, it had made one of their friend's young sons cry. He was still in Venice and was, to all accounts, making his way through the world with the usual fits and starts along the way. He would thrive because he tried.

Orazio was the most academic of his four sons. He was the one who had learned to read early, at the age of six. From then on, he had been obsessed with books and managed to weasel one from Trissino every time he saw him. Trissino had become accustomed to selecting one from his library and tucking it into his pocket before leaving to visit Palladio if he knew that Orazio was at home. At one point, Orazio had fancied himself a poet, penning a tearful longing lament for a damsel who never even looked at him, one Geronima Colonna d'Aragona.

And although Orazio was completely unlike his older brother Leonida, as a boy, he had followed him around like a puppy.

Silla, the youngest, was his favorite son. *Perhaps the youngest ones were the favored ones because they were the last and reminded the parents of their own youth*, Palladio thought. At any rate, Silla was the domesticated one who stayed close to home, knew how to make tiramisu, and was a capable rabbit skinner. Silla was the son who wanted to be useful, so he learned what needed to be learned in order to help out. Palladio knew that Silla would know where the receipts from the stonecutters were kept, when the shipment of stone would arrive, who was the most skillful baker.

And then, of course, there was Zenobia, who, as he had expected, had soon given him petite Enea and stocky Lavinia, both of whom enjoyed knee dandling.

The night was drawing down and he began to shiver from the cold. When he stood up, his knees cracked. Was it the cold or his age, he wondered, and went inside to find warmth.

Chapter Twenty-Seven

1570: COMPLETING *THE FOUR BOOKS OF ARCHITECTURE*

Palladio was in his back garden, his unpublished book in his lap. He had begun it twenty-eight years ago and it was finally finished. It was a miracle he had continued to work on it because there had been so many days when he doubted he would ever complete it. It could have been like so many of his villas—skeletons that were half finished, half baked, totally useless. *That would have been ironic*, he thought.

He loved sitting in the garden. The little square of green grass comforted him and confirmed his faith in the beauty of the natural world. Even if his buildings couldn't thrive, the trees and flowers around them infiltrated the half-built ruins and gave them a modicum of beauty, for that was what nature did.

Allegradonna had made their backyard a paradise. Although it was small and surrounded by three brick walls, it contained a lemon tree, a bed of purple pasqueflowers, some brilliant scarlet cyclamen, and pure white roses. A pearly pink bougainvillea crawled up one wall, partially obscuring the Virgin Mary who peeped out from the blossoms like the maid she was.

Palladio began to think about the concept of beauty. Did a cat think about beauty? A dog? Did all people think about beauty or just those who had the time? He thought about his butcher, a pragmatic man who could sling a cleaver like an artist. He wondered if ability was related to beauty, for his butcher could reduce the haunch of a pig into a variety of meat cuts with such style and verve it was a performance to behold.

Did a murderer understand beauty? A few years ago, he had witnessed a hanging. The man had murdered three people in a roadside robbery. He remembered looking at the man with the black sack on his head, preparing for the moment of his death, and wondering what the man had been thinking about. Is it possible that the man, or another man like him, would, at the last minute of his death, think about beauty?

What was the relationship between God and beauty? Why did people make beautiful places of worship? Why, when you entered a soaring arched cathedral, did your heart and mind turn to God? God must have designed humans with the thought of beauty firmly placed in their heads. Palladio decided that neither cats nor dogs had the capacity to understand beauty.

He plucked a pale yellow rose and managed to prick himself with its thorn. As he sucked on his finger, he thought about the link between pain and beauty. There were times in his life when he had seen something so beautiful it had resulted in a physical pain that had lodged firmly in his stomach. That had happened to him when he had stepped into the Pantheon. The rain from the oculus had been streaming down, cutting the room in two. Palladio had to sit down, for the beauty of the space had overwhelmed him. He was amazed by what these great men had made.

Made. That was the last word he had written in his opus, *The Four Books of Architecture.* Yes, that was appropriate. For what was an artist but someone who made something out of nothing? It was better than a magician producing a coin from a child's ear, for art was an act of creation. And therefore like an act of God. The moment he had that thought he pushed it out of his mind, thinking it was blasphemy. Men could not produce a work like those of God. But then he paused and drew his finger over that last word. He gave himself a sort of poetic license. Artists would never be anything like God or even the gods of ancient Rome. But they could try. Otherwise, there would be no art.

He thumbed through the hand-tied book, and as he drifted through the manuscript, he found himself connecting the words on the page with the moment in his life when he had written them. Page thirty-six was the end of the first book. The drawing at the bottom of the page was ornate with decorative vines, ribbons, and birds looking outward. He flipped through the book and landed on the illustrations of the Villa Barbaro. He could see his own private weakness on that page for there was no mention of Paolo Veronese and his considerable contribution—his paintings graced every room.

Veronese had been on the right side of right, but Palladio could not bring himself to give the painter credit where credit was due. It was a petty thing and Palladio was not proud of what he had done, but he would not change it, either. That night when Veronese had visited him after Leonida's trial, Palladio had written him out of the book. The man would go uncredited in this, his life's work.

He had organized the book into four carefully chosen smaller books. The first one was the recipe book and included all of the elements for constructing a beautiful building. He had described columns: Corinthian, Ionic. He had been specific as to their dimensions, their proportions. They needed to imitate nature and thus look like trees, thicker at the bottom than at the top. For strength and pure aesthetic visual pleasure, they needed to be a mathematically precise distance away from each other.

Each description was accompanied by intricate drawings, decorative rosettes that framed the cornices, the appropriate height of an archway, the discreet measurements of ogees, those moldings that were a combination of concave and convex shapes. He included pedestals and pavements, doors, windows, chimneys, stairs, roofs, gutters, the heights of rooms, vaults, loggias, halls. He laid down the rules and then described when they could and should be broken. Someone could take this first book and use it to build something that would be, as Vitruvius had described, *utilitas*, *firmitas*, and *venustas*.

The second book was about what could be built with these elements: houses. Houses for the religious, the merchant, the warrior. This book stepped away from the materials and focused on the larger picture. He had described houses that he had built, such as the home of Count Iseppo da Porto with its two entrances; its front half was for the family and the back half could be used to house strangers. Then there was the home of Count Ottavio Thiene, a house in the middle of the city with the first floor dedicated to shops.

Each house reflected the individual needs of the owners, both social and practical. Would they need to use part of the building for the harvest? Would they need to house unwelcome and problematic family members? He included floor plans and elevations so readers could clearly see how the plan was laid out, as well as the loggia archways, windows, and tympanum.

In reality, some of the houses had been built while others had never come to life, and still others remained half built due to misfortune, death, or disaster. One of the true disadvantages of being an architect was that some of one's artworks would never be seen, for they would never be built. But Palladio had figured out a way to preserve his designs—if not in stone, than on paper. They would live within the pages of this book.

One of the sorrows of his life was that he had never received the opportunity to build a house in Venice, but in this book, he had included what he could not accomplish in real life. He had included the "inventions"—houses that he would have built if given the chance. These inventions were the result of years of imaginative speculation. He had spent hours thinking about Venice houses—what they would look like, how they would feel, how he would build them within the specific confines of the city's narrow and winding streets. In this way, they had found a life. In some imaginative world, his palaces graced the Grand Canal, rising three stories above the busy waterway.

The third book departed from houses and addressed bridges,

piazzas, roads, basilicas, and baths. It was Palladio's dream city; he had erected Rome in his mind's eye and now brought it to life through drawings and text. He used his scrupulous measurements of the ancient Rome edifices and rebuilt them, for he had measured not only the ruined stone walls that defined the floor plans of each building, but also each small decoration he had found on every little chunk of fallen stone. He took something that had been erased by the march of time and made it solid again, if only in book form.

Public buildings continued to fascinate him. From the time he had designed the Basilica in Vicenza, the idea of buildings that could be used by the populace seemed to him the very ideal of humanism. He had spent hours meticulously drawing the Baths of Agrippa, a combination gymnasium, bath, and garden. He was so fascinated by the individual rooms and their uses that he had listed them:

A. The place where the boys were instructed.
B. The place where the girls were instructed.
C. The place where the wrestlers powdered themselves.
D. The cold bath.
E. The place where the wrestlers anointed themselves.
F. The cold room.
G. The warm room.
H. The warm room where one proceeds to the furnace.
I. The hot room, called the sweating room.
J. The laconicum (or dry sweating room).
K. The hot bath.

L. The outward portico before the entrance.

M. The outward portico before the north.

N. The xystus. The outward portico toward the south, where in the winter season the wrestlers exercised themselves.

O. The groves between two porticos.

P. The uncovered places to walk in called peridromis.

Q. The stadium, where the multitude stood to see the wrestlers engage.

R. The east.

S. The south.

T. The west.

U. The north.

The fourth book he had reserved for temples, the houses of the gods. In many ways, describing the ancient temples of Rome had been his opportunity to write about the meaning of beauty itself. Palladio had described the world as a sort of temple, an homage to God's creation, while these designs of man were diminutive attempts to recognize the greatness of God. These small attempts needed to be as beautiful and grand as possible. They were placed on hills or facing waterways, and included numerous porticos or other welcoming architecture so that people would be drawn to them like bees to honey.

As was true in the other three books, Palladio often quoted and referred to Vitruvius, giving him the recognition, respect, and honor that he deserved. He agreed with many of Vitruvius's ideas, including that round temples were the most beautiful, followed closely by the quadrangular. The round temples echoed the sun and the moon as they traveled in a vast circle across the earth. They were the best temples for they were simple, uniform, equal, strong, and capacious with no beginning and end.

The quadrangular temples were buildings that formed crosses. People could enter at the foot of the cross and travel down its length until they reached the nexus where the altar began, where the choirs would sing to the heavenly hosts, where they would receive holy communion and listen to the wise words of the priests.

Both forms required a large, welcoming, yet imposing portico. Columns would support the tympanum with an air of magnificence, grandeur, and solemnity. The materials should be as good as the religious community could afford. The feeling when one came into the portico should be a combination of awe and smallness; the color, white.

Palladio had used the quadrangular temple design when creating the San Giorgio Maggiore in Venice, and had drawn the plans for the church while remembering the tumbled stones of ancient Rome.

He rose from his chair in the garden and went inside to his desk. Using tender care, he covered the front of his book with vellum, tied it with purple silk ribbons, and then wrapped it in coarse-grained ecru paper. A work of nearly thirty years. He patted it fondly as though it were the head of a favorite dog. Three decades of painstaking drawings, illustrations, and descriptions of his life's work. He hoped it would have some impact. He hoped people would recognize it for what it was: one man's dreams, his thoughts, his opinions on all things aesthetic and materialistic. It was a recipe book for making buildings that would allow a certain expansiveness for the people who resided in them. At least he hoped so.

Chapter Twenty-Eight

1570: DEATH AND GHOSTS

Jacopo Sansovino had been ill for quite a while and Palladio had not found the time to visit him. However, news had traveled fast—Sansovino was dying. At eighty-four, his body had finally begun to fade and death was clearly imminent. Palladio had been called to Venice, to Sansovino's deathbed. He felt as though half of his life had been spent by the bedsides of people who were near death.

As Palladio walked toward Sansovino's apartment, he stopped for a moment to contemplate the clock tower that separated the religious square of St. Mark's from the fast-paced mercantile Rialto area. It was large in scale and could be seen from the water so that all boats passing by could see the time and, more importantly, see how prosperous, successful, and wealthy Venice had become. The two figures on the top terrace were especially appropriate on this day. One was old and one young, and each hour these hinged figures beat on the bronze bell to mark the passage of time. Palladio, shielding his eyes from the piercing sun, imagined that the older shepherd seemed more bent than the last time he had seen him.

The tier below featured one of Palladio's favorite icons: the winged lion of Venice. The lion represented Saint Mark, who, when traveling to the lagoon that would someday be Venice, met an angel who said to him, "*Pax tibi, Marce, evangelista meus. Hic requiescet corpus tuum.*" ("May peace be with you, Mark, my evangelist. Here your body will rest.") And indeed, his body did now rest in the basilica nearby that bore his name. Kneeling before the lion was a statue of Doge Agostino Barbarigo, a ruler who had borne the brunt of multiple warring tribes who had attempted to take over his beloved Venice.

The Virgin Mary and Jesus sat on a third tier. Twice a year—on January 6, the epiphany, when the Magi had visited the baby Jesus; and on Ascension Day, forty days after Easter—the Magi, led by an angel, paraded around the curved balcony, bowing to the Virgin Mary and her child.

And below that tier, finally, was the clock. In blue and gold, it combined the moon and the sun, astrological symbols, and Roman numerals to create a constantly shifting architectural, religious, and artistic marvel. Palladio never tired of looking at it and his gaze was in constant motion for there were so many details to take in.

He sighed suddenly, realizing why he was there. Sansovino had been a rival but also a colleague. Palladio had been called because of his book.

Sansovino's apartment was sumptuous with brocade, velvet,

marble flooring, silk tassels with knots the size of his fist, and paintings by Andrea del Sarto, with whom Sansovino had shared a studio in Florence. Palladio was especially taken with one painting in particular that rose above the vast fireplace. It was a version of the Pietà. It was a soothing portrait; the Virgin Mary's beneficent oval face radiated soft white light onto the face of Christ. As Palladio waited to see Sansovino, he took a moment to pray for the man's soul. Sansovino would soon see for himself the gates of heaven.

When Palladio was finally led into Sansovino's chambers, he sensed that his colleague had taken care in making sure the room was as pleasant as possible and that he himself was presentable. Palladio approached the large oak bed where Sansovino appeared as shrunken as an old apple, his deeply wrinkled face sprouting a gray beard that frothed down his chest. Sansovino waved him closer. Palladio neared the bed and caught a faint whiff of sourness.

Sansovino gestured him even closer, forcing Palladio to put his ear down to Sansovino's withered lips.

"My thanks, Palladio . . . the book" was all he could manage.

Palladio took his hand and gently squeezed it. He knew what Sansovino meant. In his book, he had referred to Sansovino's most ambitious, creative, and treacherous project, the Biblioteca Marciana, the library of St. Mark's. Palladio had honored him.

Palladio had been invited out to the Villa Foscari, a villa he had designed for the Foscari brothers, Nicolò and Alvise, in 1559.

He had taken the Barbaro gondola oared by his friend Luigi, the gondolier who had first brought him down the Grand Canal so long ago. As Luigi skillfully docked the gondolier, he crossed himself and kissed his thumbnail. Perhaps it was Palladio's imagination, but the villa seemed to emit an unhealthy and choking air. The gardens, which had been meticulously planned and planted, were now cloaked with weeds. The trees and bushes were untrimmed, grasses grew thigh high, and the mournful cry of a magpie cut through the stagnant air.

The building was still imposing as the Foscari brothers had requested, but Palladio did not understand why a black seeping stain cascaded from the tiled roof. Unlike many of the other villas in the area, this one was not a working farm. Instead, the brothers had wanted a place to entertain dignitaries. Palladio had built a high berm and then constructed the villa on top of it—not only to increase its sense of prestige, but also to lift it out of the spongy land. The Foscaris wanted visitors to feel the power of the family that had included Francesco Foscari, a doge who had ruled Venice for thirty-four years.

Now, however, the building would not impress a delivery boy. Even the Brenta River that had been clear and clean now seemed murky, with a stench of rotten grasses and fish.

Perhaps it was his own mood permeating the landscape, for he was there to solve a problem. That summer, when the warm rains came from the south, a small but troublesome leak had appeared on the third floor in a room where the servants lived. Several of these men and women had to be moved to another room, and the Foscaris had immediately sent word that Palladio should come to see what he could do.

This was an embarrassment, of course, since Palladio prided himself on designing buildings that would withstand the test of time, and a house that was scarcely twenty years old should not develop leaks.

Nicolò himself greeted him at the place where the two sets of grand stairs converged. Palladio thought that he, too, looked like he had sprung a few leaks for the man had a slightly watery and dissolute presence about him. Twenty years ago, Nicolò had been a strapping man of fifty with a new wife, Elisabetta Dolfin. By all accounts, Elisabetta was a wonderful wife for Nicolò—a young, vibrant widow who had come with a fine dowry.

Palladio had been at a dinner that she had hosted, and she had proven to be educated in art history, proficient at five languages, and an experienced conversationalist who put everyone at ease. She was full of youthful zest and had fiery red hair that had been pinned up with a sapphire hairpin in the shape of a peacock. Perhaps that should have been a sign; many people distrusted peacocks, believing that the males sported hundreds of evil eyes amidst the design of their feathers. Palladio had been enthralled by her storytelling and wit and left far later than he had intended.

Now, Nicolò led him to the third floor listlessly, as though drifting with the tides. Palladio examined the ceiling and realized the main wooden beam that supported it was rotted through. This meant that the leak had gone unchallenged for years. The good news was that it could be easily replaced from the outside. Palladio would call on his most trusted tilers, men he had known for years, to rip away the tiles and replace the beam.

He told Nicolò that he was lucky. If the rain had permeated into other areas, the repairs would have been extensive and costly. Nicolò ran a hand through his sparse hair nervously and coughed up a thin laugh. As they discussed what they would do, Nicolò led him back downstairs. The rooms were filled with frescoes by Battista Franco and Giovanni Battista Zelotti, all exploring Greek mythology. Every wall was filled with legends— Jupiter and Mercury witnessing a murder; King Midas sitting on his throne as naked Envy is dragged toward him by her hair. Each side room explored a theme: geometry, arithmetic, war, wisdom, music, and astrology.

Normally, these kinds of frescoes of ancient gods and goddesses with their epic tales invigorated Palladio, but for a reason he could not fathom, that day it made him grind his teeth in discomfort. As they sat together and ate grapes and cheese and discussed what to do next, Palladio thought he caught a flash of red and black in the doorway of Bellona, the goddess of war.

"Is that Elisabetta?" he asked.

Nicolò stood up abruptly, bringing the conversation to an end. Palladio was outside, breathing in the boggy air, before he had time to blink.

He shook his head and wandered down to the gondola where Luigi sat under a willow tree eating his own grapes and cheese. Not wanting to interrupt, Palladio sat down with him, insisting that he finish up before they went back to Venice.

Palladio found himself sharing the peculiar events of the day with Luigi. Luigi crossed himself again and told Palladio that people no longer referred to the villa as the Villa Foscari but rather the Villa La Malcontenta. Servants were gossips and throughout the years a terrible story had unfolded. Nicolò had accused Elisabetta of everything that a young wife would never want to be accused of: adultery, childlessness, and an unwillingness to do her wifely duty. (This last part Luigi had indicated through an intricate series of gestures.)

In one lightning-filled evening, things had come to a boil. The servants heard glass breaking as it was thrown at the walls, the rending of silk, and terrible cries. They were worried that murder was being committed. But instead, when the dawn broke, Nicolò simply said that his wife was never to set foot outside of the villa ever again. Never. And for fifteen years that was what happened. People sometimes saw her peering from the windows, but no one ever saw her in person again.

Palladio stared back at the empty windows and they stared back at him. "She stays there always?" he asked Luigi.

"No," he said, slowly shaking his head. "She is not there anymore."

Palladio frowned, feeling the hairs on the back of his neck rise. He didn't know which was worse, staring at the house or turning his back on it.

Luigi whispered, crossing himself yet again. "What you saw—"

He did not have to finish the sentence. Palladio leapt to his feet and pulled Luigi up as well. They hurried to the gondola and jumped in. Almost before he had sat down, Luigi had entered the sluggish current and they slowly drew away from the cursed place. Palladio knew that he would have to come back to supervise the repairs, but for now, all he could think about was the flash of the red-haired woman in black.

Chapter Twenty-Nine

1570: VILLA ALMERICO (LA ROTUNDA)

When Palladio was led into Paolo Almerico's study in his palace in Rome, he admired the flowing crimson curtains and the polished crushed marble floor that glinted green and blue. It reminded him of the quilt that Allegradonna had brought with her as part of her dowry. The painting by Titian that spanned the arching ceiling was filled with fabulous cherubs and angels in blues and golds, but Palladio found himself focusing on one small spaniel who sat at the knee of the angelic host.

When Almerico entered, he was so frail and thin that Palladio had to resist the temptation to grab his elbow and steer him to a chair. Almerico tottered his way to a seat behind an immense walnut desk and, breathing with difficulty, gingerly sat down. He picked up a pamphlet and started fanning himself with it. He seemed crushed by life and his shoulders sagged as though he, like Atlas, bore the burden of the world.

It was true, he had seen the worst of humanity. He had spent two years in a Venetian prison for the charge of murdering a man by the name of Bartolomeo Pagliarino. Palladio knew this wealthy nobleman, as he had received a commission from him in 1544 for a villa. The plans had fallen through, however, when Pagliarino had suddenly died. Poison was a nasty business.

After two years moldering away in a damp prison cell sharing food with the rats and becoming food for the fleas, Almerico was finally released. He stayed close to the church, assisting Pope Pius IV and then Pope Pius V, but then realized that he was through with the intrigues of religious life. He wanted to retire in a place that would be a balm that would soothe and contain him for the rest of his life.

In a thin voice, he told Palladio that thanks to his beloved father, he now owned land south of Vicenza. He was ready to retire and he wanted a building where he could entertain friends and engage in the pleasantries of farming and husbandry. He wanted something "nice," as he put it.

Palladio had done his homework. He knew that for Almerico, "nice" meant something grand. Something that would impress his friends and colleagues. Something that perhaps even God would take note of.

Almerico made it clear he was in a hurry. He wanted to live in his new domicile within a few years at most.

Palladio departed from Almerico's home admiring the tapered chandeliers and the intricately woven tapestries. He knew why Almerico was in such a rush—he wanted to live in this, his last house, before he died. Palladio would do everything he could to hurry the process along, for this was a project that he had been waiting for: a chance, at last, to build his own Pantheon.

When he went to visit the site several months later, he was thrilled. He sat in the long grass and took in the view. On one side was the Bacchiglione River, which sported a red punt carrying a load of barrels. On the other was the bounty of the land personified: vineyards, fields of wheat, lemon trees. The air brought a heady perfume of tangled grapes, citrus, black earth, and birdsong.

His mind was already racing, designing, building. For Almerico's villa, he would incorporate a dome. Over the years he had drawn many domes in many drafts, but none had survived the architectural process. This was his chance. He would design the rooms to respond to all four compass points; this would be a building where everyone would be treated equally to the wonders of the Vicenzan countryside.

Palladio sat in that one spot all day long and watched as the sun moved along the sky. He focused on one tree and sunk small sticks into the earth to record the trajectory of the shadows. Periodically, he licked his finger and held it up in the breeze to gauge which way the wind came from. He meticulously recorded his findings in a slim notebook using a small brown quill and his favorite apple ink. He would incorporate these features of natural beauty and health into the design. Each room would have access to the available breezes in the steamy summer months, and would feature a large tiled fireplace that Almerico and his friends could sit around in the cold winter months. Perhaps some of the guests would be elderly like Almerico himself. Palladio imagined them sitting in front of the roaring fire with their gnarled hands outstretched, reveling in the rosy heat that emanated from it.

Almerico wanted his palace to be grand, but he also wanted it to be a working farm, capable of bringing in income each year. He planned on selling his palace in Rome and extending the property in Vicenza so that he could produce a fine annual bounty.

Palladio would build the kitchen and the storage areas in the basement and it would be as beautiful in its own simple way as the main floor, the piano nobile. He would create an environment in white to take advantage of the light that would be indirectly seeping in from the corridors. The rooms below would echo the rooms above: four large rooms coupled to four smaller ones.

In many ways, Palladio envisioned this lower floor as his favorite, for it would be unadorned, constructed simply from light and shadow. The kitchen would be a pleasure for all who worked there—copper pans would line the walls and the stone floor would be laid in a pleasant herringbone pattern. The rest of the working areas, such as the barns and stables, would be strategically hidden from view; even the noise and smells of the necessary work would be dissipated by physical berms or buried underground.

When guests looked out of their windows they would feel as though they had entered a dream. Vineyards, framed by elegant archways and a march of columns, would be dripping with Sangiovese and Nebbiolo grapes, red-eyed patches of tomatoes, corn lined up like soldiers in structured rows, and the leafy greens of lettuce ready to be picked. Palladio hoped that visitors would imagine Ceres, the Roman goddess of the harvest, feathering her way through the scene, touching a tree that would instantly bear fruit.

When they looked up in their individual rooms they would see ceilings filled with images of Roman mythology. This was as Almerico wanted it, for he had studied mythology and iconography. If Palladio could have had his own wish, it would have been for a neutral palette. Lately he had come to believe that the sun and the moon were the best painters and would furnish any household with a constantly shifting vision that reflected God's evolving vision for mankind.

Of course, it would be the dome that would astonish. It would dominate the central core of the building. At the top would be the oculus, the eye of God. It would be open to the heavens, and when it rained, a grinning satyr in the floor would act as a drain that would pour into a central well in the floor below. Almerico wanted the dome to be splendid, a temple that gave voice to Roman mythology. Life-sized statues by Lorenzo Rubini and Giambattista Albanese would drape themselves along the main circular rim, portraying Apollo, Ares, Demeter, and Hestia, all Olympian gods and goddesses who ruled the lives of men. Diana would stand tall, ready with arrows at hand.

When guests would enter the central dome, they would invariably look up. Palladio enjoyed this thought, for he knew that architecture manipulated human behavior. He had always taken advantage of this knowledge to improve the lives of those who experienced his buildings.

Finally, as the day was drawing to a close, Palladio stood. It was time to make his way back to his own home, to Allegra-donna, who was waiting with a steaming pot of chicken stew. Although visions of the future danced in his mind, his body's need for the comforts of hearth and home were calling.

Chapter Thirty

1572: A DOUBLE SHOCK

Palladio didn't see the lone rider pounding toward him, approaching from the southeast, from the city, where his family was. He was squinting into the cold morning sun as he looked up at the workmen standing on the scaffolding. They were installing the bricks that would form a crenelated border along the top edges of the tympanum, the triangular facade of the pediment. They had begun as soon as the first rays lit Vicenza's Berici Hills to the south. He was watching carefully; he needed to ensure that the bricks were placed correctly, for there could be no errors in Paolo Almerico's new domicile. Every brick needed to be the same size. Since brick makers were paid by the brick, they were notorious for skimping and making the bricks smaller than they were supposed to be. Perfection was in the details and Palladio could spot a defective brick instantly from three stories below.

He suddenly became aware of a rhythmic sound. He

turned to see a rider savagely whipping a driven Esperia pony, approaching fast. No one would drive a horse to this extreme unless something was wrong. The horse was dripping foam from its mouth and foam flecked its sides. It was blowing hard and its nostrils flared, its exhausted breath releasing into the frosty December air in steaming clouds. The rider pulled the weary horse to a halt right in front of Palladio.

Palladio did not know the rider. The man had a sallow complexion and his face showed pock marks from a childhood disease. He fell wearily from the horse and stood before Palladio, hat in his hand, looking as though he had ridden all night. He gasped three words—"Leonida is dead!"—and Palladio's heart plummeted through the earth and broke.

Leonida, his firstborn, his most troublesome son, dead.

Details were scant. Allegradonna had dispatched the rider to find Palladio as soon as she heard.

Palladio found himself on the frozen ground, the air drained out of him. He looked out over Almerico's frozen fields. *Leonida is no longer on this earth. I will never again see his mischievous grin as he hides my favorite pen and he will never again release a pig into the house. I won't be able to scold him about his drinking habits or his propensity to involve himself with other men's wives.*

As he looked over the skeletal grape arbors and the wind driving the branches so they clacked together, the earth seemed devoid of life. But Palladio knew that under the ground, in the folds of the hoar-covered earth, it was teeming with life. Life. That curious force. That God-given animator that could be so easily taken away. An inestimably valuable quality that when gone, left only a thing that was as inanimate as a lump of clay.

He remembered when his father had died. While he contained a whisper of life, there had been a certain lightness, and even though it was not visibly apparent, a certain energy. But the second he had passed from this life to the next, his body had instantly become leaden, the blood pooling in splotches and blotches, his face sagging, almost instantly caving in, losing weight, losing vigor. And he remembered the day when his mother had died. How he had tried to snuggle next to her to gain warmth and solace, how it had been like nuzzling a stone.

Leonida should have lived through his wild days to understand the ways of life and settled down with a good woman and raised his own wild child. He should have lived until he grew old and fat . . . or old and thin. He should have had the chance to slow down and contemplate his youth and think about the error of his ways. Instead, his life had ended far too soon.

Palladio remembered the day that Leonida had been born. His worry for Allegradonna almost eclipsed his thoughts about being a father or having a son, or what he would do if he couldn't keep food in the mouth of this small new animal that had not been on this earth seconds earlier. Leonida had come out with black hair and screams. Robust and demanding. Kicking wildly with his tiny feet.

Now he was forever still. Forever quiet.

His foreman, Pasqualine, approached quietly, creeping up on Palladio's left side with his hat in his hand. He said nothing, but instead sat down next to him, staring out at the icy fields. It was bitter, this wind, and it robbed the heat from the body almost imperceptibly until the body shook. Palladio stared at his hands, chapped and red. These hands had held that baby, shaking in fear and wonder, afraid he would drop his squirming new son. Now, his hands lay inert in his lap, merely endpoints at the ends of his arms, content to stay motionless until they, too, froze up. Until they, too, died.

He felt as though he could have stayed there forever on the frozen ground. He envisioned people finding him in the spring thaw as the snow revealed a man who had simply given up and fallen asleep in grief.

But Pasqualine eventually pulled him up. Palladio managed to stand. Managed to be put on a horse. Managed to ride back into town. Managed to stumble inside his house where Allegradonna took one look at his face, wooden with cold and sadness, and sat him by the fire. Her heart was breaking, so she did the only thing she could do. She tenderly took Palladio's coat off, sat him down in front of the fire, fed him gruel laced with wine, and placed his feet into water that had been heated by the fire. Only then did she sit down next to him.

A silence came over this husband and wife, who together had built this boy, this man, who was no longer alive. They sat together until the fire died in front of them. Allegradonna looked at the embers, which resembled a small candlelit town. One by one, they flickered and were dark, then turned to ash. The room grew cold and yet the couple did not move. They sat there together in silence until cold gray morning light seeped around the shuttered window. Their Leonida was dead.

The news came in fits and flights. Details were as thin as a few words. *Sea. Boat. Tragedy. Violent. Unfortunate.* Pulled from the waves. Leonida had died over a month ago and his family still did not have a body.

And then life sent them another blow, this one compounding the first. Throughout his life, Orazio had followed in the footsteps of his older brother. When Leonida had brought tadpoles into the house and slipped them into his father's wine, Orazio had snorted in peals of supportive laughter.

In death, Orazio was no different. Scarcely a month and a half after Leonida's mysterious demise, word came to Palladio and Allegradonna that Orazio had once again followed his brother. In a rare moment of togetherness, Palladio and Allegradonna had both been at home. They had been sipping Lapsang souchong tea, a gift from Daniele, who knew that they both treasured its smoky exotic flavor. They were grieving, remembering, staring into the hearth when, again, a stranger came to call.

In response to a wild dare, Orazio, who had developed a passion for horses, had failed to jump over a fallen oak. The horse, an enormous roan, had valiantly attempted the jump but instead hit the tree, twisted aside, and landed on Orazio, instantly breaking his neck.

Two sons dead in less than three months.

～

Palladio found himself wandering the countryside, down the Valley of Silence. Like a madman who had no sense of propriety, he wrapped himself in his cloak, crawled under a drooping willow tree, and fell asleep. When he woke, the night was full on with no moon. He found his way back home in near blindness, his hands outstretched, stumbling over rocks and tree branches until he finally managed to reach his own door. Allegradonna had been worried and waiting. She brought him in with trembling hands. The morning dawned and neither of them had slept. Allegradonna went to tend to the fire; he went to his desk. The birds he had drawn looked outward, staring at something no one else could see. They could see their future.

Palladio shriveled into himself like a snail encountering salt. No work was done. No plans were planned. No drawings drawn. He took long walks that sometimes lasted a day and a night. At points, his friends and employers were so worried about him that they sent teams of boys to scour the countryside. The boys would find him sagging near a lone pine in a field of frozen wheat stalks or in an alley next to a shivering street dog. They always found him alone.

Allegradonna was the opposite. She threw herself into numbers, challenging herself with long complicated equations, burying her grief and her hands in soapy water, again and again, washing the terrazzo floor, again and again adding up numbers in her head. The grief almost destroyed both of them as they crept into their separate corners.

When Leonida's body was finally delivered to them, it was cloaked in cloth that had been soaked in vinegar and herbs to cover the spoiling. Orazio was already in the ground, and they buried Leonida by his side. Palladio designed two stones for their graves. Vines curled, roses bloomed. The stones were designed so that the vines leapt from one stone to the other. The young brothers, as they had in life, now followed each other to the afterlife.

Chapter Thirty-One

1572: A TERRIBLE SCARE

Allegradonna was not a nurse by nature. She was cerebral, not naturally nurturing, but she loved Palladio and was happy to sponge his brow and feed him until he got his strength back. But neither of them saw the toll it was taking on her. After the deaths of two of her children, she plunged herself into helping Palladio through the shock and keeping his business afloat. She was up before dawn every morning, making sure that Palladio's books were still balanced, that the masons were being paid, that the limestone was still being delivered to the right villa. She cooked broth for him, making sure that the chicken it came from was a spring chicken, not some old hen that had seen better days. She gave him sponge baths, fed the goats, tended the garden, met with potential bricklayers, reviewed floor plans, milked the cow. And then one day she collapsed, struck down by a high fever.

This fever was violent. It tossed her around, her own private earthquake. She shuddered and convulsed, and her eyes rolled back in her head. Palladio, Silla, and Zenobia took turns at her bedside so she was never alone. Palladio was terrified. It was enough to lose two of his children—must he lose his wife as well? To keep her from falling out of bed, he tied her down, using wide red silk ribbons so they would not cut into her skin.

She strained against those ribbons, the veins on her forehead pulsing with the effort, while sweat poured off her. She was often delirious, asking for her mother who had died long ago, shouting to an unseen demon who seemed to be standing directly behind Palladio, shuddering with terror as she thought that she stood on the edge of an endless chasm. In his mind was a single terrible word: plague.

But Palladio never left her side. It was three days and nights of terror. It was as though he were in a kind of cyclical nightmare: The servant brought in new water; Palladio dipped in a clean cloth, wrung it out, laid it on Allegradonna's brow; she screamed or shuddered or whispered to ghosts in the room; he tried to calm her, but she couldn't hear; and then for a short moment, she slept and he dozed. He woke when she began to mutter, and when she began to scream, he started his routine again.

However, on the third morning, a morning that was bright with birdsong, she did not wake him with screams. He woke naturally when the sun, streaming through the window, landed on his face. There was a disturbing silence and he immediately looked at Allegradonna. She looked lovingly back at him with her luminous brown eyes. The fever had broken. He untied the ribbons, took her hand, held it to his cheek, and then he sat there and cried like a child.

Chapter Thirty-Two

The news from Venice was appalling. The plague had entered the city on little cat's feet and no one was being spared. It was 1574 and the summer had been sullen and still. No wind had cooled the Grand Canal and the plague was infiltrating all levels of society from the nobleman's palace to the lowest den of squalor.

The city stank of bodies. The narrow streets were piled high with garbage and rats scampered along the eaves in broad daylight. It was a place to avoid at all costs. People who had become ill were taken to the island of Santa Maria di Nazareth, sometimes called Lazaretum, where they were placed in a bed with two or three other people. If they were fortunate enough to survive, they were transported to Lazzaretto Nuovo, a nearby island, to convalesce. The others met an unfortunate demise. Workers were kept busy from sunup to sundown, shrouding the bodies and laying them out in mass graves.

According to the news that seeped slowly out of the city, noblemen and slaves alike were laid in the grave and there had even been accounts of people who had been mistakenly flung into the graves while still alive. With difficulty, they had clawed their way out of the mass of putrid bodies, pushing aside the clammy blood-soaked hands, coming face to face with open mouths and milky unseeing eyes. It was as though one of Dante's circles of hell had come to life.

Doctors could not stem the flow of death. Mothers could not save their children. Husbands watched as their wives grew ill and died. Finally, the ruling senate declared that if God would lift the plague, they would erect a church thanking Him for His delivery.

Slowly, the plague burned itself out. In two years, it was as dead as the many that it had laid in the ground. A church would be built. The senate decided to give this critical religious chore to a group of Capuchin monks who inhabited the Island of Monks, also known as Giudecca, a long sliver of an island just off of Venice. Palladio had been awarded the opportunity to design it. He knew that his friends the Barbaros and Campani had been behind the scenes pulling strings for his benefit.

The first time that Palladio went to visit, he was amazed at the brisk winds that came off the water to brighten and freshen the journey. He was to meet the head friar, a man whose quiet reputation superseded him. As Palladio leapt from the gondola to the wharf, he almost missed and took a dunking in the Venice canal. *That would have been an auspicious beginning,* he thought as he caught his balance.

He was met by Friar Gregorio, a slender young man with fingers that fluttered around him like birds. He was barefoot and dressed in a coarse brown robe. He led Palladio into a vine-covered cloister that ended at a rough-hewn table that was set up under a mulberry tree. Friar Bianchi stood to greet him. He looked at Palladio with the clearest bright blue eyes Palladio had ever seen, eyes that seemed to look right through him. The friar gestured for him to sit and poured water into a wooden cup. He looked down at the cup and over at Palladio, who took the cup and drank. The water was better than the Venice water and he marveled at its clarity. Friar Bianchi nudged a bowl of grapes and a wooden plank that contained cheese, grapes, and bread. Palladio ate.

It wasn't until after he had stopped eating and sat back that Friar Bianchi began to talk. His voice was curiously musical and seemed to burble up and down like a lively brook.

"I am sad that my most kind and wise predecessor, Father Bernardino Ochino, is not here with us. He understood true humility before God." He crossed himself several times and ate a grape before adding, "And I have forgiven him for his Calvinist conversion."

He then went on to address the subject at hand: the design of the new church. The friar said that Palladio was a gift from God and that it was in poor taste to question gifts.

"However," he said, and Palladio thought he saw a glint of humor in the man's eyes, "I do have a few thoughts." He popped another grape into his mouth. "I trust you to create a beautiful building that will reflect the thousands of prayers thanking

God for delivering us from the plague. But this church must reflect our order. Unlike the church that is planned to the west," he said, gesturing toward the site where San Giorgio was being built, "this holy house of Christ will not hold the remains of any noblemen. It will not be a reliquary of rare and religious objects. It will not be made of expensive stone or marble or anything that resembles wealth and consumption." He wiped his eyes. "Brick and terracotta will be a better choice."

Palladio looked at him and wondered if this seemingly simple friar was actually an astute judge of character who had not only spent time researching Palladio himself, but also his way of working, his impediments, and his desires.

Friar Bianchi added that he wanted this church to "reflect reflection," as he put it. The mind and the body would be soothed by such a space, for wasn't life cruel enough?

Palladio thought back for a moment about the past few years. The loss of his blessed sons, his beloved wife almost succumbing to an unnamed fever, his architectural designs time and time again not chosen—all of these events set in front of a vast backdrop of a country suffering from a terrible plague. Yes, it was cruel. And beautiful. And terrible. And filled with harmony and discordance. It was all of these things.

"Do you know why we are called Capuchin? It is because our beloved children thought we looked like walking cups of cappuccino." On that note, he gestured and two steaming cups of creamy cappuccino appeared before them.

They talked for several more hours and Palladio found himself succumbing to a rare feeling of calm. Usually, his leg would jiggle in impatience or excitement. This day, his leg was still. Perhaps it was the courtyard itself, for they were ringed in with slender bricked porticos that protected the courtyard from any noise or other disturbances from the outside. The mulberry tree was very old with dark mature fruit that drooped from almost every branch. The branches with their three-fingered leaves hung down as though asleep.

Friar Bianchi finally pushed away from the table. Even he seemed to be reluctant to break the calm spell that had settled over them. It was rare for two people to see the world in such a similar manner. This new church—Chiesa del Santissimo Redentore (Church of the Most Holy Redeemer)—would be simple and grand at the same time. Palladio felt that it would be one of the finest designs of his life.

As the last rays of the sun disappeared behind the lacy clouds to the west, Palladio found himself on the wharf watching a gondolier manipulate the gondola that he was to take back to the city. By now, it was almost dusk and the city had calmed, turning into a pastel arrangement of soft azure and pink. The servants were beginning to light the Doge's Palace with candlelight and its many windows began winking awake. As Palladio made his way back to the city, he was already erecting the church in his mind's eye. After a lifetime of practice, he could imagine buildings and make them as real as stone even before a single drawing had been made.

Chapter Thirty-Three

1578: TEATRO OLIMPICO

Palladio scrambled over the ruin of the old prison wall and scraped his shin. He stopped to examine it. His aging skin was thin and bled easily and a trickle of blood ran down his leg and into his shoe. Palladio dabbed at it with a cloth he kept in his pocket for just such occasions.

At seventy years old, he ached from the tip of his toes to the top of his bald head. However, his mind was still sharp and for that he was grateful. God had given him a mind that was able to imagine—the most essential element for any artist, and he still had the imagination of a young man. This was a good thing because the Accademia Olimpica, the gentlemen who were his friends as well as patrons, had given him a task that filled him with eager pleasure. They had selected him to design the Teatro Olimpico, an audacious, once-in-a-lifetime opportunity, the first permanent theater in the modern world. For what was a town without a theater?

True, they had been able to mount many good productions in parks, on streets, in squares, and of course in the Basilica (including Trissino's *Sofonisba*), but the time had come to build something that would reflect Vicenza as a town of culture and prestige. A theater like this would be a statement: Within this town lived people who were thinkers, designers; people who were engaged in civic life. Unlike Rome, Venice, or Florence, Vicenza would have a permanent theater that would resonate throughout the New Roman Empire. No other city could claim one.

Pietro Porto, the president of the Accademia Olimpica, had gone to the city—specifically to the Magnifica Comunità, the men who ran the city government—for a proper place to build. In just three days they had an answer, possibly because many of the same people who were members of the Accademia Olimpica were also members of the Magnifica Comunità. They suggested a space where the old prison had been—the spot that Palladio now traversed. This spot, defined by the Bacchiglione and Retrone rivers, and across the street from the Palazzo Chiericati, was within the confines of the Castello del Territorio, a structure that had originally been built in the thirteenth century to guard access to the city over the bridge.

As Palladio climbed around the old prison, he tried to get the lay of the land. The site was narrow, challenging for a theater, especially for the design he had in mind. Some of the walls had fallen but most of them were solid. He stared at the one that veered away on his right. Palladio rather liked the intricate wall with its assortment of red hand-hewn brick interspersed with white stones, the negative spaces formed by holes, and the occasional larger white stone that protruded from the surface. It was a wall that led the eye around like a dog on a leash; first here, then there. It would add visual interest to the courtyard, a place where people could picnic before seeing the play. He envisioned the moment clearly: the audience dressed in their finest, sipping delicate wines, waiting for the swallows to come out at dusk, a clear signal that the play would soon begin.

He had in mind a *teatro all'antica*, a theater that was based on all of the ones he had scrambled over, all of those he had measured and imagined: Rome's Theatre of Marcellus, the ancient theaters he had found in Verona and Pola, and Vicenza's own Teatro Berga.

Palladio would dig down deep into his life, down into his memory, his training, his experience. He would channel Vitruvius, Trissino, Barbaro, and his own father, who so long ago pointed out the architectural details of his mill. In 1565, he had created a theatrical set out of wood. Here was his chance to make something similar out of stone. Or at least something that looked like stone.

He sat back for a moment, suddenly out of breath. For a moment he stared up at the sun and realized how many days of his life this same sun had stared down at him. What had he managed to accomplish? Buildings. Bridges. Churches. Countless villas where he had contributed his heart and soul. Some which were only partially built. Some which were still being built. Some of which would never be built. *How maudlin I've become*, he thought.

He stared at a sparrow that was hopping around a nearby rosebush. His heart turned in his chest and he thought about all who had gone to God—his father, his mother, Leonida, Orazio, Trissino, Giovanni, and countless others. When one was old, one experienced a parade of people steadily dying until one was alone. And then one joined the parade.

He looked at the ruined landscape, a place that had harbored the pain and suffering of so many prisoners. If one were lucky, life was not only made up of pain and sorrow, but also of joy. In addition to pain, he had experienced so much happiness and beauty—his marriage to Allegradonna, the birth of their children, the completion of his Villa Rotunda.

It was at that moment that he made himself a promise: He would transform this derelict and neglected space into a theater of life. He would design a place where people could experience all of it, all of life, the joy and the beauty as well as the pain and the sorrow.

It rose up solidly in his mind. In order to fit the theater into the narrow footprint, he would take Vitruvius's original concept for a theater, a geometrical circular scheme made out of four equilateral triangles, and flatten it out, making it elliptical. The audience would sit within that elliptical space and there would not be one seat that was lesser or greater than another. The pitch of the seating section, or *cavea*, would be sharp so that no one would have to lean to the side in order to peer around the high hat of the patron in front of them.

Palladio thought back to the week he had spent examining, measuring, and soaking up the Teatro Berga—the walls of statuary that had tumbled to the ground, the vastness of the sky overhead, the innate beauty of the destroyed design. Such a sad and diminished space.

Suddenly, a great idea came to him: He would honor the Berga theater that was ruined by becoming a prison. And he would do this by transforming the Castello del Territorio, a former prison, into a theater. He enjoyed this conceptual balancing of fate, even if it was something he would keep secret in his own mind.

The *cavea* would be ringed with double planes of colonnades and statuary. In honor of the Accademia Olimpica, who would be paying for most of it, the proscenium over the stage would be filled with reliefs depicting the labors of Hercules. And although this would be an indoor theater, it would have the feeling of an outdoor one; the large curved ceiling would be painted with a summer's wispy clouded sky.

It was all coming together in his mind. All theater was artifice. By design, it placed the audience into a specific time and setting. It erased their life circumstances for a duration, left them without bodies, and allowed them to wing their way to occurrences real and imagined. He would design the wall so that some of it was real and some simply a painting. It would be artifice within artifice, a kind of layering of realities.

He stared again at the ancient wall that stood before him. He could look at it all day. The theatrical space would echo the wall and be alive with images, faces, bodies, stories. It would reverberate with voices from the past and present. If the play on stage was flagging, people would be able to entertain themselves by looking at the statuary that surrounded them, and if they tired of that, there would be plenty of opportunities to simply look at the other people in the audience. It would be a place of humanity; a place where people could laugh together, perhaps weep together.

Chapter Thirty-Four

1578: ALLEGRADONNA DIES

Losing two of her children had almost killed Allegradonna and she had never regained her personal wit and spark. It had been eight years of gradual fading. Every morning she faced the day anew, trying as best she could to wrangle up some joy. Zenobia's children were the bright stars in her life and when they jumped into her lap, she almost looked like herself again. But when she and Palladio were alone, she was like a book unread. She sat there with treasure inside her that could not be discovered by any means, for it was buried in grief. The two could only sit and hold hands. Words were no longer needed and indeed seemed to get in the way.

Palladio buried his own grief in work, but the work that belonged to Allegradonna did not occupy her mind. As she washed and cooked she saw the dead as children, their mischief and laughter, the small ways they found to make her just a little angry. They crowded around her, these children—her children—who were gone forever, and there were many times when she would bury her face in her apron and pray that they would go away, as their faces were terrible to remember.

Children should not die before their parents, she always said. It is not what God intended. When she said this, Palladio took her in his arms and simply held her. Many days now, he was gone from home and he felt that he was not able to ignite a light in her eyes.

Allegradonna spent most of her days at the Vicenza Cathedral for it was dedicated to the Annunciation of the Virgin Mary, who of course understood losing a son. She said that they talked, she and Mary, about death and heaven and children and life. Sometimes, Palladio was afraid that she had gone mad, but when she would say these things, she would look at him with clarity—for grief was indeed a kind of madness, but one in which the mind was painfully aware.

Now, Palladio was at her bedside holding Allegradonna's hand. Some couples rarely touched; some could not keep their hands off each other. Palladio and Allegradonna had always been hand holders. Her hands had changed over the years and the one he held now was wizened and filled with blue-green veins, her nails ridged and void of color. "Like three-day-old fish," she said, smiling slightly as she lay there under the blue wedding quilt.

Allegradonna had been the right wife for him. Through the rigors and pleasures of five children and a life of constant movement, their marriage had been as solid as pink granite. Even through the sorrow, she had been his companion. Her grief had unbound her, but not from him.

As Palladio sat next to her bed, he thought about loss, for ultimately, all life seemed to be made up of a series of gains and then, as surely as the sun revolved around the earth, a series of losses. All eventually turned to dust.

For the last few days, Allegradonna had not been lucid, but rather sunk in an internal sleep. Yet at that moment, she opened her eyes. She smiled at Palladio, and for an instant, he remembered when he first saw her, her eyes not willing to break away from his. All the years had now dropped away, for her eyes penetrated into his soul.

"I see them," she said, squeezed his hand, and then simply stopped breathing.

He sat there for hours. When Palladio finally stepped out into the street, it felt as though he took his first real breath from the moment Allegradonna had taken her last. He breathed in the morning air, gray and chilling before the dawn. People were just starting to stir, and the rolling sound of the first carts and the nickering horses and the crowing of roosters began.

Perhaps it was not about loss after all, but a kind of eternal clock, like the wheels on the cart that rolled by him, loaded with fresh hay. For wouldn't there always be new people to replace the old, new buildings on top of old ones, new days that followed the ones before? He felt a coolness on his cheek—tears rolled down his face and he thought of them like small rivulets that must traverse the country of his beard and the many creases of his face. He stretched, for his bones ached, and he went to find the priest who had given Allegradonna her last rites.

Chapter Thirty-Five

1580: THE DEATH OF PALLADIO

Palladio walked from his home to his studio each day. He treasured this time alone, for most of his day was now busied by important people who wanted his time, and time was becoming more and more precious. Lately, he tired easily. When he took the spiral staircase in Chiericati's house, he felt winded. Even now, as he walked along the narrow streets of Vicenza, he realized that he was slowing down.

Perhaps this was not all bad. It would allow him to more perfectly study every window, every door, every spanning arch and lintel. Perhaps he would slow down so much he could watch as the ivy slowly crept its way up a carving of Venetian stone. The sun and the moon would cast their slow paths each day and he would sit in a corner and watch the shadows on the plaza slowly match their arc. He would observe the pigeons with their comic operas of marriage and children. He would take time for Zenobia's lovely children, his grandchildren.

As he rounded a corner, noting a painting of the Virgin Mary painted on the wall ahead, he felt a sudden jolt in his chest. A searing pain lanced across his torso and he felt as though he were being torn in two. Before he knew it, he had spun to the ground and was looking up at the sky. He heard flapping that echoed against the buildings. A pigeon flew overhead and disappeared out of his field of vision. A breeze freshened his face and lifted a pale wisp of hair. *He would have time*, he thought. He would have time to do all of these things.

He had delivered the plans for the Teatro Olimpico to the Accademia only yesterday. They had received them well; he remembered seeing only the tops of their heads as they pored over the intricate drawings. Their voices were a constant murmur until someone would spot some fine detail and point it out. Then their voices would dart like fish, gathering around the detail.

He focused on the corner of a building, three stories up. A statue stared down at him. *Hercules*, he thought. The Accademia had adopted Hercules not only as their patron, but as a sort of role model—and Palladio had decided to incorporate a series of reliefs above the theater's proscenium arch depicting his challenges. He recalled the Accademia's rallying cry, "And now comes the hard part."

How appropriate, he thought, *for life was a series of struggles.* He had prevailed through recalcitrant noblemen, violent children, premature deaths, pestilence, and pain. He knew he had, in some small way, made something of his life. If he were lucky, his buildings would last for a time, and neither wars nor politics would tear them down. They would continue, he hoped, to give pleasure to those who saw them and lived in them. *They would continue to slow the restless heart and open the troubled mind,* he thought.

And then Palladio gently passed away.

Afterword

Stand in the middle of any intersection in the Western world and try to find a building where Palladio has not had some influence—staircases, arches, theaters, banks, hallways, doors, windows, barns, stables. Once I understood the design elements that defined "Palladianism," a style of architecture credited to Andrea Palladio, I began to think about how much one person can change the world.

Palladio was that person who had the rare combination of technical skills, emotional intelligence, imagination, artistic acumen, and luck. By all accounts he was a man of honor, an excellent dinner companion, and an exceptional architect with an eye for beauty, an ear for harmony, and an innate understanding of materials and men.

All architects are tender thieves, for when they see something they like, they steal. Palladio was an exceptionally discerning thief, one who became fascinated with the styles of ancient

Rome, had the skill to translate them, and had the ability to improve upon them.

He was working during the Italian Renaissance, a time when Italy was alive with curious people who were involved in pushing the current boundaries and asking the question of "What if?" Mathematicians, astronomers, painters, poets, and composers were feeding off of each other, building a wave of new ideas that were embraced and amplified.

Although ongoing wars, personal tragedies, and family intrigue would often compete for the personal coffers that funded Palladio's buildings, many of these structures succeeded in being built. The rest of the plans existed only as drawings in his book, but each one rose like a phoenix because architects became enamored with those plans—they were simple in their classicism and classic in their simplicity. The lines spoke from the page and people recognized elegant designs that could be used in everything from city buildings to residences.

If you have the good fortune to find yourself in Vicenza, Italy, you will experience an entire town that is not only the home of more than twenty buildings directly attributed to Palladio, but also filled with structures that were built after he died, buildings that resonate with the Palladian style. It is a town built with Ionic columns, rooftop statuary, and collections of successive arches. Banks, children's clothing stores, bookstores, restaurants, cafés, residences, garages, cloisters, and churches are all housed within his architecture. It is nirvana for architects: Every building is a calming, glorious series of shapes that encourages one to breathe more deeply. Vicenza is rain pouring out of elegant spouts, steps that fit the body, and expansive windows that look out onto the Valley of Silence.

And if you can venture out into the surrounding countryside, you will have the opportunity to view some of Palladio's master works, villas he built for the noblemen who wished to make their mark upon the world. They are places that combine beauty and utility, that rise from the green fields and country roads and pronounce themselves works of art.

Palladio was rare in that he was a commoner who succeeded in becoming an architect. This happened because his life was filled with people who supported him. They introduced him to influential people who had money and a desire for excellent residences, and to religious figures who needed beautiful churches to celebrate the glory of God. He was never wealthy, but his ability to "walk with kings—nor lose the common touch" (Rudyard Kipling) served him well, for he could communicate equally well with masons and stone cutters, priests and noblemen.

As I researched this book and traversed the streets he walked upon, I grew to love Palladio. I held his 1570 edition of *The Four Books of Architecture* in my hands. The careful printing and hand binding made me want to be there when he wrote the last word. I wanted to be at the table with his friends while they deliberated over philosophy, military strategy, poetry, and theater. I wanted to be able to peek over his shoulder as he carefully drew the elevations of his imagined buildings.

Goethe, the famous German writer, said this about Palladio:

"*Ein recht innerlich und von innen heraus grosser Mensch.*" (A righteous man inside and a great man from inside out.) Note the word *mensch*.

I hope this book honors the life of Andrea Palladio. After reading about him, you won't be able to walk down any street without seeing his spirit clearly represented by the lintels, the rooflines, the geometric shapes of the buildings around you. Understanding Palladio gave me a new way to look at the world. I hope it does the same for you.

Palladio's Legacy

On December 6, 2010, the U.S. Congress recognized Palladio as the "father" of American architecture. Given that America is a huge country filled with brilliant architects as varied as Frank Lloyd Wright, Julia Morgan, Louis Sullivan, and I. M. Pei, how is this possible?

It's probable that it is all due to his book, *The Four Books of Architecture*, which Palladio published in 1570, ten years before he died. This beautifully illustrated book is both magical and practical.

Around 1660, Inigo Jones, the English architect, came to Italy and saw Palladio's buildings. There is evidence that he bought a copy of Palladio's famous book. One thing is for certain: Jones, as well as William Kent and Lord Burlington, saw the designs of Palladio and Vitruvius, and echoed Palladio's ideas in such important buildings as St. Paul's Cathedral in Covent Garden, the Queen's House at Greenwich, the Banqueting

House in the Palace of Whitehall, and the Queen's Chapel in St. James Place.

Although most of Palladio's influence is seen in Europe, in 1699 his book found itself in Russia via Prince Dolgorukov. Unexpectedly, Palladio's designs impacted the most common of abodes, the country house.

In America, Thomas Jefferson took up the charge, designing not only one of his own plantations, Monticello, but the Rotunda at the University of Virginia, which looks strikingly like Palladio's own Villa Rotunda. The rotunda as a design choice raced around the country like the latest craze, including at Duke University, John Hopkins University, Syracuse University, the Green at the University of Delaware, the University of Illinois, Florida State University, and Vanderbilt University. Even Tsinghua University in Beijing built rotunda buildings on their campuses.

From there, Palladio's designs became ubiquitous. Pavilions, suburban houses, even dollhouses have reflected his classic Roman styles. Architects and builders whose names have faded from history recognized good design and capitalized on it. The Palladian style is so common as to be rendered almost invisible.

Perhaps less known is Palladio's ability to see limitations as opportunities for new design concepts. Time and time again, he would take a site that was too wet, too narrow, too hampered by constraints, and turn the building into something special. His solutions to the problems became the defining characteristics that set the designs apart from other buildings of the day.

Not only was he a talented architect living at the right time and place, but he was also special in that he was a man who embraced the sixteenth-century concept of humanism. Perhaps this was because he exemplified it. The basic tenet of humanism is that all citizens should be able to read and write, to be exposed to the finer arts such as theater and poetry, to be able to speak clearly and with distinction, and to participate in civic life. He was able to do all of these things even though he was born into a lower class. Although he befriended nobles and priests, it is very likely that he knew what it was like to go hungry, and as far as anyone knows, he never owned a house.

The miller's son rose to greatness and changed the landscape by translating classic design and making it his own. He thought about the people who would live in his buildings. He imagined their lives and the lives of their ancestors. He built for the future, and 500 years later, many of his buildings still stand.

His buildings in Vicenza and his villas are now on the World Heritage list, which means that they are protected under the Decreto Legislativo 42/2004 and cannot be changed without authorization. Palladio's buildings join other irreplaceable natural and manmade structures such as the Pyramids of Egypt, the Great Barrier Reef in Australia, and the baroque cathedrals of Latin America. The World Heritage sites are under the protection of the United Nations and are considered to belong to all people of the world, no matter where they are located. I think that Palladio would approve.

About the Author

Pamela Winfrey is an award-winning writer and curator.

As a writer, she specializes in writing surreal plays for a thinking audience. She is especially interested in the relationship between theater, reality, science, surrealism and mental health issues. She has received funding from the Sloan Foundation and the Marin Arts Council and was a finalist at Arts and Letters. She won an award at the Method and Madness Festival in Denton, Texas, and her work received the Audience Favorite and Best Actress awards at Variations Theater in Manhattan. Her plays have been seen as far away as Toronto and Ireland. She was one of the founding members of Mobius Operandi, an electro-acoustic sound sculpture ensemble and performance company which produced five large-scale, walk-through, site-specific performance pieces in San Francisco. She is also the author of *Marconi and His Muses: A Novel Based on the Life of Guglielmo Marconi.*

As a curator, Pamela represented the United States in the Interactive Art Panel at Ars Electronica (Linz), was the lead curatorial consultant for Emerging Artforms for Creative Capital, and curated more than 100 exhibitions, performances, artworks, and installations at the Exploratorium in San Francisco, where she is senior artist emeritus. She was the co-curator for the West Gallery, a gallery which explores human phenomena, and curated "The Changing Face of What is Normal," an exhibition on mental health that was dear to her heart. She has a BA in theater, an MA in interdisciplinary arts, and is currently getting her MFA in screenwriting from Stephens College.

www.pamelawinfrey.com

Dark Labyrinth
A Novel Based on the Life of Galileo Galilei
by Peter David Myers

Defying Danger
A Novel Based on the Life of Father Matteo Ricci
by Nicole Gregory

The Divine Proportions of Luca Pacioli
A Novel Based on the Life of Luca Pacioli
by W. A. W. Parker

Dreams of Discovery
A Novel Based on the Life of the Explorer John Cabot
by Jule Selbo

The Faithful
A Novel Based on the Life of Giuseppe Verdi
by Collin Mitchell

Fermi's Gifts
A Novel Based on the Life of Enrico Fermi
by Kate Fuglei

First Among Equals
A Novel Based on the Life of Cosimo de' Medici
by Francesco Massaccesi

God's Messenger
The Astounding Achievements of Mother Cabrini
A Novel Based on the Life of Mother Frances X. Cabrini
by Nicole Gregory

Grace Notes
A Novel Based on the Life of Henry Mancini
by Stacia Raymond

Harvesting the American Dream
A Novel Based on the Life of Ernest Gallo
by Karen Richardson

Humble Servant of Truth
A Novel Based on the Life of Thomas Aquinas
by Margaret O'Reilly

Leonardo's Secret
A Novel Based on the Life of Leonardo da Vinci
by Peter David Myers

Little by Little We Won
A Novel Based on the Life of Angela Bambace
by Peg A. Lamphier, PhD

The Making of a Prince
A Novel Based on the Life of Niccolò Machiavelli
by Maurizio Marmorstein

A Man of Action Saving Liberty
A Novel Based on the Life of Giuseppe Garibaldi
by Rosanne Welch, PhD

Marconi and His Muses
A Novel Based on the Life of Guglielmo Marconi
by Pamela Winfrey

No Person Above the Law
A Novel Based on the Life of Judge John J. Sirica
by Cynthia Cooper

Relentless Visionary: Alessandro Volta
by Michael Berick

Ride Into the Sun
A Novel Based on the Life of Scipio Africanus
by Patric Verrone

Saving the Republic
A Novel Based on the Life of Marcus Cicero
by Eric D. Martin

Soldier, Diplomat, Archaeologist
A Novel Based on the Bold Life of Louis Palma di Cesnola
by Peg A. Lamphier, PhD

The Soul of a Child
A Novel Based on the Life of Maria Montessori
by Kate Fuglei

For more information on these titles and
the Mentoris Project, please visit
www.mentorisproject.org